Diallo's soldiers mounted a desperate assault

They came on like a banzai charge of old, shouting and with weapons a-blazing. Mansaré's people were fighting for their lives at odds of three to one.

Bolan hurled frag grenades against the charging line. The cops blasted through the ranks, but they were taking hits, too. The men who'd stretched prone on the ground to fire their autorifles whittled down the other side, until silence finally reigned.

One of the "dead" men stirred behind Mansaré, rising on his elbows to extend a pistol. The shot from Bolan's FAL drilled into the back-shooter's skull, drawing all eyes to the soldier's position.

The Executioner rose slowly. "We need to talk."

2006 34
2010 17
2013

MACK BOLAN ®
The Executioner

The Executioner®
Don Pendleton's
ROGUE ASSAULT

A GOLD EAGLE BOOK FROM
W❂RLDWIDE®

TORONTO • NEW YORK • LONDON
AMSTERDAM • PARIS • SYDNEY • HAMBURG
STOCKHOLM • ATHENS • TOKYO • MILAN
MADRID • WARSAW • BUDAPEST • AUCKLAND

Recycling programs
for this product may
not exist in your area.

First edition August 2013

ISBN-13: 978-0-373-64417-9

Special thanks and acknowledgment to
Mike Newton for his contribution to this work.

ROGUE ASSAULT

Printed in U.S.A.

Conflict is created by two conditions: the evil that is sanctioned by the corrupted…and the sacrifice borne by upright men and women who choose to destroy it.

—Adam Turquine, from
Beyond Mars Crimson Fleet

We draw a line and say "No farther," but we never find two lines in the same place. Today I draw another line and make a stand. A sacrifice. Whose blood? Only tomorrow knows.

—Mack Bolan

THE
MACK BOLAN
LEGEND

Nothing less than a war could have fashioned the destiny of the man called Mack Bolan. Bolan earned the Executioner title in the jungle hell of Vietnam.

But this soldier also wore another name—Sergeant Mercy. He was so tagged because of the compassion he showed to wounded comrades-in-arms and Vietnamese civilians.

Mack Bolan's second tour of duty ended prematurely when he was given emergency leave to return home and bury his family, victims of the Mob. Then he declared a one-man war against the Mafia.

He confronted the Families head-on from coast to coast, and soon a hope of victory began to appear. But Bolan had broken society's every rule. That same society started gunning for this elusive warrior—to no avail.

So Bolan was offered amnesty to work within the system against terrorism. This time, as an employee of Uncle Sam, Bolan became Colonel John Phoenix. With a command center at Stony Man Farm in Virginia, he and his new allies—Able Team and Phoenix Force—waged relentless war on a new adversary: the KGB.

But when his one true love, April Rose, died at the hands of the Soviet terror machine, Bolan severed all ties with Establishment authority.

Now, after a lengthy lone-wolf struggle and much soul-searching, the Executioner has agreed to enter an "arm's-length" alliance with his government once more, reserving the right to pursue personal missions in his Everlasting War.

Prologue

East 142nd Street, South Bronx, New York City

"Is it just me," Clay Hollister inquired, "or is this neighborhood the shits?"

"It's not just you," said Devon Lang, hunched down beside him in the DEA surveillance van.

"I didn't think so," Hollister replied. "But you know how I like to be politically correct."

"Yeah, right." Lang's smirk was almost audible.

Hollister couldn't say the South Bronx was the worst place that he'd seen in sixteen years of service as a drug enforcement agent, but it absolutely ranked among the bottom four or five. Some of the district's blocks reminded him of photos taken in Berlin, after the bombing raids of World War II, except the old-school Nazis hadn't scrawled graffiti on their ruins. And, the last he'd heard, they didn't spend much time killing each other in the streets.

Okay, some parts of the South Bronx were livable, but only just. Hollister wouldn't want to spend a night in any of the tenements he'd seen so far. Between the roaches, rodents and the roving gangs, he didn't see how any decent person could relax enough to sleep. A place like this, he thought, you either made escaping from the ghetto your life's work, or else you gave up as a kid and let it pull you down.

"It's time," Lang said.

Hollister spoke into the mouthpiece of his wireless headset. "Entry teams, report."

"Team A in place and ready," said the stolid voice of Special Agent David Jones.

"Team B, ditto," SA Rick Patterson chimed in.

The second-floor apartment they were raiding was a stash house, nothing cooking, if his information was correct, but Hollister had called up members of the DEA's Clandestine Laboratory Enforcement Team just in case. One thing you could predict about drug traffickers: the pricks were unpredictable.

"Hit it!" he ordered, rising as he spoke and moving toward the van's back door. He had already sweated through his T-shirt underneath the Kevlar vest with DEA printed in yellow on the chest and back. It was like putting on a target, and the vest was only large enough to help him if he took a slug between the collarbone and navel. His head, neck, arms and everything below the waist was totally exposed, the vest a mere illusion of security.

Hollister hit the street with Lang behind him, trusting in their driver to prevent some local punk from ripping off the van. That would look great in Hollister's report: a hundred grand and change in rolling stock evaporating while he tried to grab a handful of West Africans and—what?—fifteen or twenty kilos of coke?

Hollister felt a hundred pairs of hostile eyes tracking his progress as he crossed the street, detouring around a junker with its wheels gone and windows smashed, and hit the lobby of his target tenement. Upstairs, he heard a door crash, shouting, then the hammering of guns.

MAMADOU CISSOKO WISHED there could have been some warning that the cops were coming. At home, he knew the price of things and who to ask about connections, but the law seemed unapproachable to him in New York City. Part of that, he knew, was that the men in charge were mostly white and made no secret of their personal contempt for Africans, Asians—outsiders, in a word. Beyond that, he wouldn't have known how much to offer, whether he was being robbed or treated to a discount rate.

And now, he realized, it would have made no difference in any case. The officers stampeding through his flat weren't local police, but federal agents, their vests, jackets and caps emblazoned with initials for the U.S. Drug Enforcement Administration.

Cissoko's only saving grace was that he always tried to be prepared. Within an hour of arriving in the States, he had acquired his first black-market firearm, building up his arsenal as cash flowed through his hands, always prepared to fight—and die, if need be—to protect his interests and his family. While not well educated, he had memorized the penalties for cocaine trafficking in the United States: ten years to life in prison for a first offense involving five kilograms or more.

And there were thirty kilograms in Mamadou Cissoko's shabby bedroom, bagged and ready for delivery.

The moment that he heard the raiders shouting, as his door came down, Cissoko grabbed the mini-Uzi that he always kept within arm's reach and sprayed the doorway with a stream of 9 mm Parabellum slugs. He saw one agent drop, leaving a puff of crimson mist behind, and looked around for Victor Kalabane. He saw him charging from the small apartment's tiny bathroom, hoisting khaki trousers with his left hand while the right brandished a .50-caliber Desert Eagle.

The raiders opened fire, then, automatic rifles chattering, stitching erratic patterns on the dirty walls. Cissoko dived behind the swaybacked sofa, lunging for the hatbox where he kept the hand grenades.

A little something extra for the Feds, to see what they were made of.

He yanked the pin from one grenade and lobbed the bomb toward the doorway, followed quickly by another, then reached up and blindly fired off the remainder of his mini-Uzi's magazine to keep them scrambling for the last few seconds of their lives.

The double blast was music to Cissoko's ears.

Cackling, his SMG reloaded, he leaped up and charged the enemy. He saw Victor sprawled off to his left, where slugs or shrapnel had come close to disemboweling him. No matter. They would meet again in hell, and soon, if there was such a place.

Laughing manically and firing on the run, Cissoko rushed to meet his death.

Osvaldo Vieira International Airport, Guinea-Bissau

Mack Bolan left the air-conditioned cocoon of his TAP Portugal flight from Lisbon and stepped into bedlam. The airport's smallish terminal was crowded almost to the point of overflowing, damp air crackling with nervous energy. A babel of voices assaulted his ears as he wound through the crush of bodies, forging a path toward the decrepit-looking baggage carousels.

Osvaldo Vieira was the only international airport in Guinea-Bissau, clinging to its designation by virtue of scheduled flights to Lisbon, Casablanca in Morocco, and Dakar in Senegal. Its single asphalt runway greeted four airlines only, and TAP Portugal's flights made the trip only three times per week. Passengers bound for Dakar aboard Cabo Verde Airlines had the choice of flying on Monday or Thursday.

Mildly surprised when his suitcase appeared on the carousel's sluggish conveyor belt, Bolan retrieved it, showed it to a yawning attendant and moved off to collect his ride. Two agencies controlled car rentals at the airport, and he'd picked the one because they claimed to try harder. Someone apparently had failed to tell the local staff, three women seemingly infected with the same near-narcolepsy as the baggage watcher.

Drawn away from sluggish conversation with her coworkers and clearly resentful of it, Bolan's clerk took eons to retrieve his reservation from a computer so neglected that cobwebs fluttered around its fan duct. She managed to discover it at last, to the relief of other Lisbon passengers lined up and muttering behind him. There was no question of challenging his paperwork—all in the name of "Matthew Cooper"—although the woman spent enough time reading it that Bolan wondered if she was committing it to memory.

His car was one of last year's Peugeot 308s, a four-door family car whose silver paint had faded to something like battleship gray. That suited Bolan perfectly, as it would make him less conspicuous. Already a visible stranger in Guinea-Bissau, where 99 percent of all inhabitants were black and most of the rest were mixed-blood mestizos, Bolan needed all the cover he could get.

The car ran well enough, once he'd received the keys, located it and shown his rental contract to a scowling security guard who appeared to find it suspicious. Bolan thought the guard might try to walk him back inside the terminal, but finally he grunted and moved on to glower at the next driver in line.

The airport was small enough to make escaping from its clutches relatively simple. Bolan wedged his car into a river of departing traffic and followed its flow southwestward on the Bissauzhino highway to the heart of Guinea-Bissau's capital and largest city. Established as a Portuguese fortress and trading center in 1687, Bissau had shipped thousands of slaves to the New World over the next 120 years, before the traffic was banned by rival nations with superior navies. Today, ships departing from its harbor on the Geba River estuary carried peanuts, copra, hardwoods, rubber, palm oil—and cocaine. Many of the city's estimated 407,500 inhabitants lived in abject poverty, a trait shared with their countrymen in smaller cities, towns and rural villages.

The smell of war was inescapable in Guinea-Bissau. Rebels had formed the African Party for the Independence of Guinea and Cape Verde to expel their Portuguese masters in 1956, touching off a seventeen-year struggle that succeeded only when a coup d'état in Lisbon toppled Portugal's military junta in April 1974. A revolutionary council ruled for the next decade, hunting and slaughtering those who had opposed the rebellion, filling mass graves at Cumerá, Portogole and Mansabá. Guinea-Bissau held its first multiparty elections in 1994, then saw President João Bernardo Vieira challenged by a military coup four years later, touching off a year-long civil war. Vieira's forces won that round, but only briefly; a second coup deposed him in May 1999. Vieira's successor, President Kumba Ialá, left office at gunpoint in September 2003, victim of another coup, later returning to seize the presidential palace briefly in May 2005. Voters gave João Vieira another chance as president in June 2005, but army assassins removed him forever in March 2009, placing his top aides under house arrest.

The smell of blood and gunpowder, in short, was everywhere.

And Bolan would be adding to it soon.

His first stop in Bissau was an auto junkyard on Avenida do Brasil, a few hundred yards from the port's waterfront. Bolan nosed his Peugeot in among the rusting hulks of older cars battered to hell and back by years of hard driving or seconds of crushing impact, killed its engine and stepped out. A dog the size of a small pony came to greet him, padding silently on oily dirt, and sat six feet in front of him, its yellow teeth fully displayed.

An old stoop-shouldered man came next, ignored the dog and spoke to Bolan with a gravel voice. "English?"

Uncertain whether he was asking nationality or preference of language, Bolan said, "American."

After digesting that, the man asked him, "You want to leave that car?"

"I'm here to buy, not sell," Bolan replied. "I was referred to you for certain special tools."

"Referred *por quem?*" the older man inquired. "By whom?"

Bolan pronounced a name he had been given before he left the States. The fellow it belonged to was a total stranger, but he was available to vouch for Bolan if the dealer called to check him out. A number in Dakar, where Bolan was advised that someone could be reached around the clock.

The dealer didn't bother, seeming satisfied to hear the name alone. "I may have what you need," he said, "depending on your preference. If you will follow me…" He turned, not waiting for his visitor to speak. He muttered something to the dog in passing and the animal took off, soon lost from sight among the crumpled and corroded cars.

The dealer's combination home, garage and office was a mobile home flanked by a line of prefab huts. He led Bolan around the west end of the dwelling, to the first hut on that side, and used two different keys on heavy padlocks that secured its door. A switch turned on fluorescent fixtures bolted to the ceiling, and a noise inside the hut resolved itself into the humming of two dehumidifiers, one planted at each end of the hut's interior.

Between them, racks and tables gleamed with oily gunmetal, while crates of ammunition and accessories were stacked along both of the hut's longer walls. The dealer shut them in once Bolan was across the threshold. He made a vague pass over his assembled merchandise with one dark hand and said, "If you find something suitable, we will discuss the price."

Bolan went shopping.

The dealer's merchandise was heavy on hardware used by his homeland's armed forces, salted with exotic foreign items here and there. Whenever feasible on foreign soil, Bolan preferred to use the local army's weapons, on the theory that their ammo was more readily available, and ditching them wouldn't point to a foreign shooter.

Bearing that in mind, his first pick was a Belgian FAL 50.63 assault rifle manufactured by Fabrique Nationale d'Herstal. It was the paratrooper's model, with a folding stock and charging handle, plus a 406 mm barrel compared to the parent rifle's 533 mm. Chambered for 7.62 mm NATO rounds, it was still a killer at 330 yards, with a full-auto cyclic fire rate of 650 rounds per minute.

For his sidearm, Bolan chose another Fabrique Nationale product, the FNP-9, chambered for 9 mm Parabellum ammunition. Its magazine held sixteen rounds, while its double/single-action mechanism let him fire a seventeenth from the chamber without cocking the external hammer. A polymer frame reduced the pistol's unloaded weight to 24.7 ounces. Tritium-illuminated sights aided with shooting in the dark, and the gun's muzzle was threaded to accommodate a suppressor, which Bolan added to his shopping list.

His third acquisition was an RPG-7, the Guinea-Bissau army's standard issue antitank weapon, with a mixed bag of high explosive, fragmentation and thermobaric rockets. The latter was commonly known as a "fuel-air bomb," because it fed on oxygen from its surroundings to produce a fiery blast wave of longer duration than any produced by condensed explosives. With an effective range of 220 yards and a theoretical striking range five times that, the RPG would open any doors that slammed in Bolan's face.

For closer work, Bolan chose a dozen M-312 hand grenades, fragmentation models copied outright from the American M-26 with its four-to-five-second fuse, plus a half dozen M-84 stun grenades. And for the closest work imaginable, he picked out a German-made KM2000 fighting knife, its 6.8-inch westernized tanto blade jet black, fitted with an ergonomic ambidextrous polyamide handle.

He paid for the lot with cash from one of his usual sources— a lowlife back home who had no further need for money—and packed his new arsenal in two sturdy duffel bags. Rolling out of the junkyard, he felt fully dressed for the first time since boarding his outward-bound flight in the States.

Zona Industrial, Bissau

BOLAN'S FIRST TARGET was a former factory located in Bissau's industrial zone, a half mile northwest of the former U.S. embassy, which had suspended operations back in 1998 and moved its people to Dakar. Officially, that meant Americans unwise enough to take their holidays in Guinea-Bissau were, at a bare minimum, 230 miles from any kind of help.

No problem. Bolan wasn't on vacation, and he had a knack for solving problems on his own.

In fact, for human predators, he *was* the problem. And a fatal one, at that.

Bolan had no idea what had been manufactured at the run-down plant standing in front of him, nor did he care. According to the information he'd received, it was a cocaine cutting plant today. The drugs came in by ship, unloaded at the waterfront and then were trucked a few blocks inland to be cut, repackaged and distributed for local street sales. It wasn't the core of Guinea-Bissau's drug network by any means, but Bolan had to start somewhere.

He counted half a dozen cars outside the factory, sedans and SUVs. If they'd been loaded on arrival there could be upward of twenty people in the old three-story building. The cars would all belong to management or soldiers, since the mean income of citizens of Guinea-Bissau topped out around five hundred U.S. dollars per year. Add worker bees, and Bolan could be facing fifty, maybe sixty people in the factory, but most of them would be unarmed and disinclined to die protecting someone else's drugs.

He hoped so, anyway.

The easy path would be to stand well back and hit the plant with RPGs, one high-explosive round to open up the brick wall facing him, then follow with a thermobaric warhead that would gut the place from top to bottom, sending all its product up in smoke. Simple. He'd take the overlords and soldiers anytime, but Bolan had no taste for slaughtering civilians who were driven by poverty into lives of relatively petty crime. He hoped they would be wise enough to flee, survive and carry word of what they'd seen back to their neighborhoods, let fear create a labor shortage for the men in charge.

While Bolan tracked them down.

Before he left the Peugeot, Bolan checked his weapons. Made a small adjustment to the shoulder rig he'd purchased with the FNP, for comfort, and made sure the thumb-break strap retaining it in place would open at his touch. He didn't need the sound suppressor this time around, knowing that once he made his move inside the plant, all hell was going to break loose.

His rifle wasn't quite so easy to conceal, but Bolan did his best. With folded stock, it measured twenty-nine inches from muzzle to pistol grip, reaching midthigh when slung by its sling. The lightweight jacket Bolan wore to hide his shoulder holster covered most of it, his hand helping to mask the barrel when he stood upright. Pedestrians were sparse on this gray stretch of road, and the soldier figured any that he met would likely focus on his white face, rather than the gun barrel protruding from beneath his jacket's hem.

Ready, he left the car, locked it and moved out toward the brooding factory.

BRUNO CABRAL WAS BORED. Guarding the plant was tiresome duty, not because of any physical exertion, but the very opposite. His shift consisted of observing peasants as they mixed cocaine with baking soda, cutting purity from 99 percent to half of that or less, and packaged the new mixture for sale to users, all without allowing them to sample any of the product or remove it from the premises. His staff of guards, nine men in all, helped Cabral watch the *cortadores*—cutters—while they worked, but also served as a deterrent against rivals who might seek to raid the factory and make off with its powdered gold.

Given a choice, which he wasn't, Cabral would happily have played the other role. There was a rush beyond the reach of any drug in stalking enemies, raiding their strongholds, robbing them, relieving them of life's sweet burden in a blaze of gunfire. Every minute that he spent eyeballing drones was precious time forever lost, nor did it help that most of them were women, stripped to skimpy underwear as one more hedge against employee pilferage. The skin show had enticed him, once upon a time, but it was dreary now.

Not that Cabral had any choice. Orders were given; he obeyed. The men behind his syndicate merely had to wish him dead, and he would be a fading memory. There was no profit in rebellion, only death and hundreds—thousands—waiting for a chance to take his place.

So he would suffer through the boredom, make the best of it and pray to all the gods of mayhem that his next assignment proved more interesting. Meanwhile…

"Inacio!" he called out, to his second in command on watch-dog duty.

"I'm coming," came the answer, footsteps drawing closer, clacking on the concrete floor.

Inacio Viegas was a stout man, muscle under fat, with a thick mustache and hair that brushed his shoulders. He wore a stubby Steyr TMP machine pistol around his neck as if it were a pendant, the eleven-inch weapon resting lightly on his belly. The arrangement left his hands free if he chose to draw the Walther PPS pistol that rode his right hip, or the long knife that he carried to the left.

"Time to have a look around outside," Cabral instructed.

"I'm on my way," Viegas said, and left the tiny office where Cabral retreated when the tedium became too much for him. He had a little television there, tuned at the moment to RTP África, airing a football game between the Guinea-Bissau national team and the Lions of Teranga, out of Senegal. Cabral wasn't an avid sports enthusiast per se, but he had bet ten thousand West African CFA francs on the match and wanted to see it play out.

Another way to kill some time.

Cabral supposed Viegas would find nothing out of place while touring the factory's perimeter. Although the threat of hijacking was ever present, business had been relatively calm in Bissau for the past six months; another truce was in place between the rival warlords. Until next time, anyway, when some insult or trespass set the blood flowing again.

Cabral supposed it was a mark of sickness that he wished something would happen, anything, to give his daily life some added spice. Money was fine, of course, but if the truth be told, he had cast his lot for the organization in hope of finding some adventure. War was bad for business, he realized, but it was also where the action was.

Without it, he was simply killing time. And time was slowly killing him.

The Lions scored another goal, their fans went wild and Cabral cursed his home team's goalie.

"You useless son of a bitch! Your mother—"

He might have added more but never got the chance, as gunfire rattled through the factory and brought him lurching upright from his chair. He snatched the AK-47 from its place beside the TV set.

THE BACK DOOR to the factory was locked, but Bolan got it open in a little under thirty seconds, thankful that the plant's chief of security was lax on hardware. Likewise, there was no alarm tape on the door or any of the windows that he could see, suggesting that the operators of the plant put all their faith in men and guns.

Why wouldn't they?

Their country had been fighting one domestic battle or another for the past half century, decades before most of them were alive. The gun, grenade, vendetta—it was all they knew.

It made them dangerous.

Once inside the factory, he shut the door behind him, softly, moving along corridors where paint flaked off the walls like scales of eczema and littered the linoleum beneath his feet. No one had given any thought to sweeping up in recent memory, letting the place slowly disintegrate as long as roof and walls remained intact. If they were breached, presumably the syndicate could find another abandoned old place to serve its needs, with no great inconvenience to the men in charge.

The soldier hadn't traveled far into the plant when his ears picked up a distant sound of music, something with a Latin tone, but something tribal going on behind the melody. He recognized that there were lyrics, but he couldn't translate them.

No matter. Tunes meant people. When he found the music's source, he would have targets.

But it didn't quite work out that way.

Bolan was getting closer to his destination, still another turn or two through mildew-smelling hallways left to go, when he picked out a closer sound. Footsteps were approaching, and a male voice was trying to sing along with the recording in the background. If the guy had asked Bolan's opinion, the soldier would have told him not to quit his day job.

Which, he saw a moment later, had to be plant security.

Bolan was looking for a place to hide—a recessed doorway, anything—but hadn't found one when the singing man came into view. He had long hair, a mustache and some kind of little SMG hanging around his neck, backing a pistol and a knife belted around his waist. At sight of the intruder, rifle raised and sighted on his chest, the guy quit singing, blinked and made his move.

He tried for the submachine gun, and reached it just as Bolan fired, drilling his sternum with a 7.62 mm NATO round from twenty feet. Even dying as he fell, the guard emptied his magazine, filling the corridor with ricochets and concrete shards while the Executioner hit the floor and stayed there, waiting out the storm.

Too close. Too loud. No more advantage of surprise.

Bolan was up and running while the echoes from that fusillade of auto-fire still rattled through the factory. However many guards remained inside the plant, they'd all be on alert now. And the hired help? Would they flee or freeze in place? Maybe retreat to something like a panic room?

Another corner, and he ran head-on into a pack of women wearing scanty underclothes and nothing else. No time to count, but Bolan guessed there had to be twenty-five or thirty, anyway. One of them squealed, and then the whole group started yelping. Bolan stepped off to one side, tried to wave them past him toward the exit, but a few in front turned back to run away from him and it became a cellulite stampede.

Damn it!

He followed, hanging back a little so that any guards the women met in flight wouldn't see Bolan bringing up the rear and fire into their ranks. It was the best that he could do right now, in terms of granting mercy to the worker bees—and as he soon found out, it didn't help at all.

The leaders of the pack had reached another turn in the corridor and screamed their way around it, all their sisters following, when automatic fire was suddenly unleashed somewhere in front of them. Two guns, at least, and in the narrow hallway it would be impossible to miss a charging crowd. The cries of panic mingled now with wails of pain and sounds of bullets ripping into flesh.

And now, like something from a British bedroom farce gone wrong—*Scarface* meets Benny Hill—the women came stampeding back toward Bolan, some spattered with blood from others, two or three clutching at wounds and sobbing as they ran. He flattened against one wall to let them pass, his rifle aimed downrange in case the shooters followed.

But the sound of screams and bare feet slapping concrete faded, and the gunmen didn't appear. Some kind of argument was going on around the corner, possibly involving the slaughter of the innocents, while Bolan edged his way along the corridor. He heard two voices, which confirmed his guess about the guns.

He pulled a fragmentation grenade out of a jacket pocket, yanked the pin and pitched the lethal egg. It made a perfect bank shot off the facing wall and was gone.

2

Mack Bolan strolled along North Randolph Street, outside the Ballston Common Mall, past trees that sprouted from their sidewalk gaps to shade the avenue. He'd been around the block already, killing time, since he had left his rented Chevy in the mall's vast parking lot, and could have rattled off the local landmarks if there'd been a quiz.

Inside the mall, if Bolan had been interested, he would have found no end of stores, banks, theaters and restaurants, all air-conditioned for his pleasure and collaborating to relieve him of his cash. He would have fit in all right, well groomed and stylishly attired, though desperately short of "bling." In fact, however, this wasn't a shopping trip, and Bolan hadn't come to see a movie. He was waiting for a ride, hoping that Hal Brognola would arrive on time.

Four minutes left.

In Arlington, they normally connected at the cemetery, strolling past the graves of heroes while Brognola sketched the outlines of the latest mission, aiming Bolan like a missile toward another pack of human predators. The dead were cool about it, never interrupting, maybe eavesdropping—who really knew?—but making no suggestions, pro or con. The choice was always Bolan's, and he rarely took a pass.

This day, for reasons that might later be explained, the big

Fed had suggested that he pick up Bolan on the street, discuss their business on the move. It made no difference to the soldier, and he trusted his old friend implicitly. Whatever his old friend might have in mind, it wouldn't be a one-way ride.

Traffic on Randolph ran both ways, the southbound lanes on Bolan's side. Brognola had to come from one direction or the other, and if Bolan had to cross the street to meet him, that was fine. He'd let the man be his tour guide, listen to whatever was on his mind and then decide where they should go from there.

Brognola had been FBI when Bolan met him, in another life and war, when the Executioner was a one-man army taking on the Mafia. It had begun as payback for his slaughtered family, then turned into an international crusade when Bolan realized that taking out one nest of vipers barely scratched the surface of an ancient evil feeding off of civilized society. His struggle paralleled Brognola's efforts to defeat the Mob by legal means, and they'd collaborated for a time, until it suited Bolan's purposes to die in public and be resurrected as a brand-new soldier with a wider war in front of him. These days, Brognola rode a desk at the Justice Department down on Pennsylvania Avenue, and answered to the Oval Office rather than the Hoover Building down the block.

And Bolan's enemies? Well, faces changed and motives varied—politics, religion, race or plain old greed—but on the inside, they were all the same: ruthless and cruel, contemptuous of human life and suffering. The only language that they understood was violence—and Bolan spoke it fluently.

In theory, his arrangement with Brognola granted Bolan freedom to reject missions that he felt to be misguided, ill-conceived or striving toward some goal that he objected to. In practice, Bolan had declined no more than two or three jobs since the program was inaugurated, one of those because he needed private time to help his sole surviving relative, the others targeting selected foreign heads of state who had displeased one or another multinational money machine.

Bolan was lethal and had earned his label as the Executioner the plain old-fashioned way, but he was not a hit man for the filthy rich.

Brognola generally screened out dirty jobs without referring them to Bolan, but he served the government, relied on it for covert funding and was forced to deal with parasites from time to time. That was a fact of life in politics, and the primary reason Bolan shunned political involvements like the plague. He had been lucky so far, but he didn't want to think about what might become of the Stony Man Farm organization when Hal Brognola eventually retired.

A horn beeped twice behind him, not the kind of blaring he'd expect to signal road rage. Bolan stopped and faced northward, just as Brognola pulled up beside him in a pearl-gray Lincoln Town Car. Bolan went to meet him, slid into the shotgun seat and settled back as the big Fed merged his vehicle with the flow of midday traffic. He turned onto North Glebe Road, taking them past colleges on either side and into the residential suburbs.

"Nice ride," Bolan said.

"Thank Javier Christos de Luna," Brognola replied.

"I would," Bolan said, "but I never heard of him."

"He used to be a big cheese with the Gulf Cartel," Brognola said. "Poor baby's doing forty-five to life, with forfeiture of assets. I called dibs on this, over a yacht."

"Good choice," Bolan allowed. "You know a boat's nothing but a hole in the water—"

"—that you throw money into," Brognola finished. "I hear you. Besides, where in hell would I park it?"

Bolan let that go, waiting for his old friend to settle in and get around to business. They were coming up on Woodlawn Park and Highway 66, the interchange, when the big Fed said, "What it is, okay, we've got a problem in West Africa."

Brognola ran it down, trusting Bolan to hear and absorb on the first pass, picking out the crucial details. Later, for the background, he could watch the DVD the big Fed had secured in the vehicle's glove compartment. And the rest of it, what followed after…well, Bolan would work that out once he was on the scene.

"It's Guinea-Bissau," Brognola said. "Not a name you hear in conversation every day."

"Or every year," Bolan replied.

"Used to be Portuguese Guinea," Brognola pressed on, "aka the Slave Coast, so no doubts about the state of race relations there. Fast-forward some four hundred years, and France grabs part of the package for French West Africa, but our President Grant weighs in to help Lisbon hang on to the rest, including a passel of islands. Natives start fighting for independence in the 1950s, but it takes them twenty years to pull it off. Since then, they mostly fight each other to decide whether they'll have a president, a military junta or some mixed-up combination of the two."

"Sounds like a mess," Bolan observed.

"It's Africa," Brognola said. "We can go back and blame the European empires, slavers, missionaries—take your pick. Or maybe it's the same damn mess we have worldwide, where races and religions clash."

"Is it a tribal thing?" Bolan inquired.

"I won't pretend to understand it all," Brognola said. "From what I understand, there are at least six mainland ethnic groups, divided by their languages and traditions, plus mestizos with some Portuguese ancestry. In terms of religion, about half the people are Muslim, forty percent or so are traditional animists and the remainder are Christians. Muslims pitched in with the Portuguese to bury an animist uprising back in the old days, around World War I, but some people are still pissed about it."

"Economics?" Bolan asked him.

"Mostly agricultural, exporting fish and nuts, which barely keeps the country going. Every year Guinea-Bissau comes in near the bottom for gross domestic product, same thing on the Human Development Index. Average household income hangs around five hundred dollars a year, and whatever the state makes from exports isn't trickling down."

"It never does," Bolan observed.

"The trouble that concerns us," Brognola went on, "began back in 2005."

"What happened then?"

"Colombian and Mexican cartels decided that West Africa would make a great transshipment point for cocaine on its way to Europe. Three years later, the chief of the United Nations Office on Drugs and Crime called Guinea-Bissau Africa's first narco-state."

"It's that bad?" Bolan asked.

"Picture this," the big Fed replied. "They have sixty-three federal officers in the whole country, to police fourteen thousand square miles on the mainland and hundreds of islands offshore. *Sixty-three* agents watching 1.7 million people. And get this—no prison."

Bolan smiled at that and shook his head, apparently left speechless.

"It gets worse," Brognola told him. "Since their last half-assed coup, back in 2010, the heads of their army, navy and air force have been designated as prime targets under the U.S. Drug Kingpin Act. Of course, we can't touch them legally, and their own government couldn't clean house if it wanted to. In September 2011 the prime minister went begging in New York, asking the UN and the European Union to patrol his country's borders. The guy can't do it himself, for fear of touching off another coup."

"I'm guessing we wouldn't be talking if that had worked out," Bolan said.

"You're guessing correctly. Twelve years and counting in Afghanistan, eight-plus in Iraq and Libya still cooking with the NATO intervention, no one in Wonderland's up for policing West Africa. As for the EU, it's too busy keeping Greece afloat. The governors see what's been happening on our side of the pond, from Bogotá to Mexico, and who in hell would want that kind of mayhem on the Continent?"

"Which leaves us…where?" Bolan asked.

"In hot water," Hal replied. "Last week, the DEA went after some Guinea-Bissauan traffickers in the South Bronx. It turned into a bloodbath. Now the White House has widows and senators howling for retribution, with no legal way to deliver."

"I get it."

"You've got it," Brognola said, "if you think you can handle it."

"Tackle the army, navy *and* the air force?" Bolan smiled again. "Why not?"

"Only the army, this time," the big Fed replied. "One general and his assorted scumbag cronies."

"Hey, sounds like a piece of cake."

"There's a DVD in the glove compartment. Should have all the details that you need," Brognola said.

"When do I leave?"

"The day after tomorrow," Brognola replied "Did I mention that the only flights to Guinea-Bissau leave from Lisbon twice a week?"

Washington Dulles International Airport

BOLAN DROPPED HIS RENTED CAR and checked into the Marriott Hotel for an easy walk to the terminal. He booked his flight to Madrid on Aer Lingus, seven hours and forty minutes nonstop, with a two-hour layover at Madrid-Barajas Airport. From there, Iberia would carry him to Lisbon on a forty-minute commuter hop, leaving Bolan with a day and night to kill before a four-hour flight to Bissau with TAP Portugal.

The Marriott was perfect for his overnight, before he flew halfway around the world to tackle the Guinea-Bissauan army and its narco cohorts single-handed. Bolan didn't feel intimidated by the odds against him, but he knew that preparation was a soldier's best life insurance. Dining on room service steak and potatoes, he fired up the DVD Brognola had provided and got his first look at the enemy.

General Ismael Diallo stood five foot nine and weighed two hundred pounds, straining the seams of his tailored uniform. As bald as a billiard ball, he almost seemed to glisten in the photos the big Fed provided, as if freshly oiled or prone to epic perspiration. He loved decorations, from the dozen medals on his chest to the Parmigiani Bugatti Type 370 watch on his wrist that retailed for a cool two hundred grand. That clearly didn't fit a soldier's salary, particularly in a country that spent less than ten million per year on all its armed forces combined. In most of the photos Diallo was smiling, smug and self-satisfied, but one caught him scowling at the camera, his face like a grouper homing on prey.

According to Diallo's file from Stony Man, he had joined the army at sixteen with his parents' permission, and had risen through the ranks with an uncanny flair for picking winners in his homeland's various coups, mutinies and upheavals. Already a general when the army moved against the prime minister in 2010, Diallo had emerged from that crisis and the European Union's halfhearted effort to reform Guinea-Bissauan security forces as de facto commander in chief of the nation's army. Despite his nominal subordination to civilian leaders in Bissau, Diallo ruled his roost, as did commanders of the navy and air force, cooperating when they felt like it, all looking out primarily for Number One.

Diallo's closest civilian ally was Edouard Camara, a veteran narcotics trafficker at age thirty-two, well connected to Colombia's Norte del Valle Cartel, based in Valle del Cauca, and Mexico's La Familia Michoacána. Both were capable of shipping cocaine by the ton, and the Mexican outfit also had a profitable sideline in heroin. He had been convicted twice in Senegal for smuggling drugs, but managed to escape both times, killing a policeman in his second jailbreak. Senegal's parliament had abolished capital punishment in 2004, but DEA reports indicated that Camara still took care when crossing the border.

In Guinea-Bissau, of course, he had nothing to fear. Brognola had exaggerated slightly about the country having no prisons. In fact, its first—an aged colonial mansion oddly dubbed "First Squadron"—had begun receiving prisoners in 1999. It hardly mattered, though, since the facility lacked beds, electric power, running water, bars or locks. With only a commander and two unarmed guards on duty, inmates routinely walked away from the so-called lockup, returning if and when they felt like it. The United Nations was collaborating with Guinea-Bissau's ministry of justice to "rehabilitate" a couple old Portuguese colonial prisons, but progress was sluggish at best.

One of the stumbling blocks, according to Brognola's file, was Minister of the Interior Pascal Kinte, a cohort of Diallo's and Camara's who'd grown wealthy by turning a blind eye to Guinea-Bissau's thriving drug trade. An equal-opportunity grafter, he also worked with leaders of the navy and air force to keep the coke flowing, but Kinte seemed to have a special soft spot for Diallo. As his dossier explained it, Diallo had protected Kinte and his family during the upheavals of 2008 through 2010, accepting Kinte's aid with smuggling as a form of payback. Not that Kinte was complaining, judging from the huge smile that he wore in every photograph available. His bank accounts in Austria and Switzerland, while maybe not as fat as General Diallo's, guaranteed that Kinte and his heirs would never want for anything.

Except, perhaps, for sanctuary from the Executioner.

None of the players knew a storm was coming, and if warned, they likely would have scoffed at any threat from one lone man. Others before them had adopted that same attitude, and all of them were dead.

Still, it would be a challenge, taking on a whole army in a nation so far gone that there were no controls over the military. And police would be a problem, too. Pascal Kinte controlled one unit, called the Special Intervention Force, whose members were suspected of assassinating officers from the rival Judicial Police, Guinea-Bissau's equivalent of the FBI, with sixty-three surviving agents nationwide. Bolan had long ago sworn that he'd never kill a cop, no matter how corrupt, brutal or murderous that officer might be. It was the only limitation that he'd set on the conduct of his private wars, but it wasn't sacrosanct. There had been an exception....

So he'd avoid police if possible. And if it *wasn't* possible...

well, he would have to wait and see what happened next. But soldiers were fair game, and Bolan reckoned he would likely bag his limit soon.

Unless they got him first.

Aboard Aer Lingus Flight 6963

BOLAN FLEW BUSINESS CLASS, courtesy of Tyrone Reeves, a Baltimore banker who had recently quit the business and dropped out of sight. He'd be a long time coming back, and Bolan doubted whether anyone would miss him much. It was a cutthroat business, after all, and swimming with the sharks in Tyrone's case had been a literal experience, involving a one-way cruise into Chesapeake Bay.

Bolan liked business class for its leg room, ignoring the bit about free checked baggage and "restaurant class" dining service. On a long trip like the flight from Dulles to Madrid, it was worth twelve hundred dollars of a dead man's money to relax and sleep in relative comfort, preparing himself for the action ahead. He couldn't fault the food, had definitely eaten worse on planes and on the ground, but it was only fuel for the machine. By this time on Friday, he'd be on the ground in Guinea-Bissau, fighting for his life.

ON RARE OCCASIONS, Bolan thought back to a time when his entire life hadn't been consumed by war or preparation for war. Those early days weren't forgotten, but they blurred sometimes, losing their color like a faded set of Polaroid pictures. He picked out images of family, all gone except for his brother, Johnny, who no longer resembled the boy he had been before tragedy struck. Friends from high school were faces with names that got lost in the shuffle, mere whispers faint to his ears.

Regrets? He had a few, as Old Blue Eyes once sang, but Bolan kept them to himself. The life he led had been a conscious choice, and he had no regrets for that. His failures—being too late for a friend in need on more than one occasion—had been balanced out, at least to some extent, by vengeance wreaked upon their killers. If the final tally ran against him…well, what of it?

Bolan understood the arguments for pacifism, recognized the courage and sincerity of champions who faced the bayonets and guns with nothing but a song and faith that human goodness would prevail someday. He honored anyone who showed that kind of valor—but it wasn't his way of confronting evil. He'd been trained by experts in the U.S. Army Special Forces, and had quit the service when it couldn't help avenge his family. The rest was bloodstained history, and Bolan offered no apology to anyone alive or dead for what he'd done.

Or for what he *would* do, if granted time, in battles yet unfought, against new enemies as yet unknown.

He browsed *Cara,* the airline's in-flight magazine, skimming an article on ancient Irish castles, one on hiking and a profile of a TV chef he'd never heard of. None of it meant much to Bolan, though he found the castle photos pleasing in a way he couldn't quite explain. Their sense of permanence, perhaps, withstanding sieges spanning centuries, now welcoming the tourist trade with perfect stoicism.

During other flights to combat zones, he'd worried about being met by hostiles on arrival. There was precious little chance of that this time, but once he had boots on the ground in Africa, Bolan knew he'd be swimming hard against the tide. Tourism wasn't big in Guinea-Bissau, as a hefty Euromonitor report would tell you for the modest price of $1,900. Bolan didn't need to spend that much of Tyrone Reeve's money to discover that the nation's poverty, endemic violence and thriving narco trade discouraged idle visitors from Europe and the States.

Why fly halfway around the world to sleep in lousy digs and get your ass shot off?

Long story short, it meant that he'd be on his own, the odd man out. More so than usual, in fact, because he'd make an easy mark for racial profiling. But he had worked in Africa before and lived to tell the tale—or not, in fact, since nearly everything he did was highly classified.

The quicker he could wrap things up in Guinea-Bissau, Bolan understood, the better were his chances of survival. Moving on to yet another battle in his endless war. That prospect might discourage some, but Bolan found it hopeful. When so many occupants of Planet Earth were simply killing time, the Executioner made time to kill.

And would, as long as time remained.

3

Zona Industrial, Bissau
Now

The frag grenade's explosion had a stunning impact at close quarters. Bolan, crouching with his face averted, heard the shrapnel slapping into cinder blocks and flesh, men crying out in pain where they'd been muttering a moment earlier. He surged around the corner, following his rifle's lead, and found two shooters writhing on the concrete floor, surrounding walls and ceiling decorated with their blood and flesh.

He kicked their guns away and left them dying at their own pace, stepping past them and the women they had gunned down, following the corridor they'd guarded with their lives to see what waited for him next. More voices drew him onward, women wailing, angry men trying to quiet them by shouting.

All too late.

More feet approached as he neared the next sharp turn, and Bolan slowed to let his adversaries close the gap. It sounded like another pair of shooters, smart enough to keep their mouths shut, but they couldn't keep their shoes from scuffle-flapping on the concrete floor. Bolan imagined them approaching, heard them slowing as they neared the corner. He crouched and held his rifle ready, muzzle leveled some twelve inches from the point where any moving target should appear.

The scouts had stopped now. They were whispering, inaudible and untranslatable, but Bolan knew what they were saying. Someone had to peek around the corner first, and they were arguing, deciding who would literally stick his neck out to discover if the coast was clear. Another beat, and Bolan heard one of the bodies shifting forward, fabric sliding against cinder blocks, until a pie-slice of a face slid into view, one eye revealed.

Bolan fired into it, a blur of crimson marking impact as the partial face slammed backward, out of frame. A startled cry reached the Executioner's ears from number two, followed immediately by a burst of auto-fire that didn't come within ten feet of his position. Panicked footsteps fled along the hallway, and Bolan slid out to see the runner making tracks in search of cover.

He was still a dozen paces from the next bend in the corridor when Bolan shot him in the back. There was no room for chivalry in combat, where you took the shots that came your way or died regretting it. His round went home between the fleeing gunman's shoulder blades and punched his target forward, airborne for an instant before facial impact with the concrete floor. From there, it was a long slide to oblivion, oiled by the blood spray from a ragged exit wound.

BOLAN STOOD UP and moved forward, careful not to leave his footprints in the fresh blood of his enemies. It didn't matter in forensic terms, considering the state of Guinea-Bissau's scientific law enforcement, but a track indexed its maker's height and stride, two clues that Bolan planned on keeping to himself if possible.

Granted, the women who had seen him and survived could tell police he was a white man, if they stuck around to speak with any officers. And if they were believed, considering the state of raw hysterics generated by the murder of their coworkers. On balance, Bolan thought he should be good so far, provided that he left no witnesses among the men who ran the cutting plant.

No problem there, since scorched earth had been the plan to start with.

Bolan hadn't seen the last of his opponents yet. More voices told him that, before a grating order silenced them. By then, he knew approximately where to find them, though he couldn't say how many rooms he'd have to clear beforehand. If the shooters who remained weren't evacuating—and he knew damned well they wouldn't call the police—he still had time. How much was anybody's guess.

Sooner was generally best in battle. Find the opposition before they found you. Kill them before they could react. Get out before you had to deal with reinforcements or authorities off-limits to the use of deadly force. But haste made waste sometimes, and it could *get* him wasted, if he didn't temper speed with caution.

Bolan moved with purpose, taking care to mask his footsteps, as he closed in on the enemy.

"BRUNO'S GOING TO BE ANGRY," Kumba Mané said. "We're late again."

"Bruno can kiss my ass," Fidelis Teixeira replied as he switched off the old Mercedes CL's engine and palmed the key. "He's never on time once, when it's his turn to relieve us."

"I'm just telling you—"

"To hell with him," Teixeira said, supremely indifferent to the moods of Bruno Cabral.

The new shift had arrived in two vehicles, Teixeira and Mané in Teixeira's Benz, five others in a black Daewoo Winstorm SUV. All carried automatic weapons in plain view, secure in the knowledge that the cutting plant had no immediate neighbors and police patrols were nonexistent in the Zona Industrial.

Teixeira checked his watch and verified that they were, in fact, some fifteen minutes late to start their shift. Cabral might bitch about it, but Teixeira doubted that he would be fool enough to lodge a formal complaint with their boss. If he did...

"The door's unlocked," Mané announced, sounding surprised.

"Stupid bastards," Teixeira said with a sneer. Now he *knew* there would be no complaint from Cabral, since he or one of his lackeys had breached fundamental security. In fact—

Mané opened the door, and Teixeira heard the sharp echo of gunfire coming from somewhere inside. In the space of a heartbeat, he raised his Kalashnikov, thumbed off its safety and shouldered past Mané to enter the plant.

"Call for backup," he ordered, and moved on inside.

The place was under attack, but by whom? There were no police cars out front, and besides, they'd been paid to stay clear, hadn't they? Who else would risk the wrath of Edouard Camara and General Diallo by staging a raid on the plant? Was it a move by someone from the navy or the air force, seeking to consolidate their hold over the drug trade?

If it was, they'd picked the wrong night for a raid. Fidelis Teixeira took it as a personal affront, and he intended to repay that slight in blood.

But he would not go rushing in and risk his life before he had at least some grasp of what was happening. Continued firing meant that some of Cabral's men, at least, were still alive and fighting to repel invaders, but for all that Teixeira knew, they might be heavily outnumbered. Then again—

Not only were police cars missing from the parking lot out front, there had been *no* cars that Teixeira didn't recognize. He could have named the owners if his mind wasn't awhirl with doubts and questions, but the names were unimportant now. How had the enemies approached, if not on wheels? Had they parked elsewhere in the zone and crept up on the plant in darkness, hugging shadows, to avoid a premature collision with Cabral's watchmen?

But if Cabral had lookouts in place, why were his enemies *inside* the factory? He should have held them at the doors and phoned for help, instead of fighting on alone against the odds.

What odds? Time to find out.

Teixeira glanced back, saw five men trailing him into the plant, while Mané talked on his cell phone at the threshold. It would take some time to pull another team together and get them on the road, but in the meantime Teixeira's people might be able to surprise the sons of bitches who dared trespass on the Family's turf. It would be good for Teixeira if he had the problem solved before more help arrived, proof of his skill and courage.

It would also work against Bruno Cabral, assuming he was still alive inside the plant.

And who said that the little weasel had to *stay* alive?

The rivalry between Cabral and Teixeira dated back five years or more. Teixeira had a chance to settle it this night, and who would be able to say which weapon had fired the fatal shot when chaos reigned?

Smiling now, Fidelis Teixeira moved more rapidly into the plant, tracking the sounds of war.

BOLAN REACHED ANOTHER CORNER, paused and listened, then peered around it. Twenty feet in front of him an open door revealed long tables in a spacious room, with jumbo plastic bags of powder waiting to be cut and parceled out into tiny envelopes for maximum returns. Shadows of movement under the fluorescent lights told him the room was occupied, but Bolan couldn't tell by whom or by how many.

Four guns down, so far, and six cars parked out front. How many guards were likely to be overseeing operations on the graveyard shift? From what he'd heard on his approach, at least two or three more.

With hostages?

It was a toss-up, Bolan thought. There might be workers in the room before him, but their masters had no reason to believe that they were dealing with police. A rival syndicate wouldn't care whether cutters at the plant survived or not, so they'd have no value as human shields. Clearing them out was still a problem for the Executioner, however, and the only answer he could think of at the moment was a stun grenade.

Voices stopped Bolan with his right hand in his jacket pocket, cradling an M-84. The startling part was that the noise came from *behind* him, where he'd thought that there were only corpses left. Two possibilities immediately registered: either police had been called in somehow, against all odds, or reinforcements for his adversaries had arrived.

Bad news, in either case, but one scenario still gave him room to fight. The other limited his options to the stun grenade and blind luck, or surrender. Call it nearly certain death.

He waited long enough to hear one of the new arrivals shouting out a question, and what sounded like an answer came back from the cutting room. Not cops, then. So his only worry was the fact that they'd surrounded him with unknown numbers, cutting off retreat.

Okay. Plan B.

He pulled the stun grenade out of his pocket, freed its pin and pitched the bomb underhand through the open doorway to the cutting room. Excited voices came from there, but Bolan was already turning back in the direction he had come from, putting space between himself and the concussive blast that he expected within five…four…three…two…

When it came, most of the shock wave was contained within the cutting room, as planned. Curses and squeals told Bolan there were men and women in the room, lost in a cocaine fog from the explosion. Did the cutters have their masks on? Did he even care?

Not much.

The major threat to his survival lay in front of Bolan now, blocking his exit from the factory. He didn't know how many reinforcements were advancing toward him, but it would take only one shooter—good, or simply lucky—to take Bolan down.

His edge: he knew that they were coming, while the opposition still had no idea exactly what was going on. It wasn't much, but he'd made do with less in other situations where the outlook had been bleak. Audacity had served him well before, when adversaries thought they had the upper hand and couldn't lose.

When trapped, he *always* came out fighting. Giving up had never been an option in the warrior's heart or mind.

Whatever happened in the next few moments, he would face it as the Executioner.

NILSON MEDINA HADN'T COUNTED on a firefight when he drew the short straw for guard duty at the cutting plant. It was supposed to be another boring graveyard shift, watching the women mix and package the cocaine without incident, unless Teixeira saw a woman that he liked and took her in the back room for a little relaxation. Nothing new or unexpected, thank you very much.

Now, here he was, creeping along with Kumba Mané and the others, trailing Teixeira as they homed in on the sounds of battle echoing from somewhere deeper in the factory. Medina clutched the dual pistol grips of his Spectre M4 submachine gun with sweaty palms, bemused that his mouth, by contrast, felt painfully dry. He recognized the nervous symptoms, tried to keep a straight face, hoping his anxiety wouldn't be visible to any of his comrades.

In the present circumstance, a doubt concerning his ability to fight could get him killed.

And if he had to kill, what then?

Cross that bridge when you come to it, he thought, which could be any minute now.

The Camara Family had accepted him based on his record: five arrests and one detention at First Squadron, where he had escaped his second night in custody. His third arrest included a charge of suspected murder, discharged without trial. Medina had a story for that case, as with the other charges he had faced: a gambling debt unpaid, resulting in a scuffle that had ended when he drew a knife and sank its blade between the debtor's ribs.

It was a lie, but no one bothered checking, since Guinea-Bissau had the highest per capita murder rate in West Africa. Medina's story of the slaying had been satisfactory, the real-life victim gutted in an alley by some killer still unknown to the police—and, more important, to his employers.

If they knew the truth…

Medina heard more shooting, and their leader moved more quickly, clearly anxious for the battle to be joined. Teixeira would be glad to rescue Cabral and his men from danger, just so he could rub Cabral's nose in it till the end of time.

But they were already too late for some. Medina grimaced
as they passed the corpses of three women barely dressed in
bloodstained underwear. The cutters had been shot at close
range, and Medina saw their likely killers as he stepped around
the corner, following Teixeira. One of them he recognized,
Francisco Gomes, staring at the ceiling overhead with lifeless,
dusty-looking eyes. His killer had been firing *past* the fallen
women, after Gomes and his fallen comrade shot them, facing death head-on.

A moment later, two more bodies. These, it seemed, were
taken down with some kind of explosive charge. Their ragged
wounds, and the erratic bloodstains on the wall and ceiling, told
the grisly story without words. Medina had seen worse, but he
hadn't been forced to step in it before. He nearly gagged, but
caught himself in time and swallowed back the acid rush of bile.

What next? Who was responsible?

Not the police. There would be vehicles out front, with
flashing lights; they would have heard the agents shouting
for a cease-fire and surrender. And police wouldn't be here,
in any case. The Special Intervention Force supported the Camara Family, while the Judicial Police were spread too thin to
mount a major raid without sufficient preparation to allow for
crucial leaks.

So, someone else.

Medina felt a little better now. If he was forced to use his
weapon, it would be against a gang of thugs much like his own
companions. He could justify it to himself, live with it, hopefully without losing what little sleep he still enjoyed. If it had
been police…

They'd nearly reached the cutting room. One final turn and
one more stretch of corridor to go. Teixeira called to Cabral
from concealment, "What's going on?"

Cabral didn't have a chance to reply. Teixeira's question was
still hanging in the smoky air when an explosion rocked the
plant, its shock wave feeling like a pair of hands slapping Medina's ears. He winced, sidestepped to give himself an open field

of fire, but there were still three men in front of him. They'd have to move or drop before the Spectre M4 did him any good.

"We're going," Teixeira said, glancing around with hard eyes, making certain everyone was with him. Nodding like the rest, Medina braced himself to charge around the corner, facing God knew what, and prove himself once more to these men whom he called his brothers.

Time to do or die, he thought.

BOLAN RODE THE SHOCK WAVE of his stun grenade toward the enemies moving to cut off his line of retreat. He couldn't say the cutting plant was out of business, but he had disrupted it at least, and likely ruined most of one full shipment from Colombia or Mexico. His next priority was getting out, to carry on the battle in Bissau and teach his targets that they weren't invincible.

Which meant staying alive.

His one advantage now would be uncertainty among the reinforcements. Whether they'd been called specifically to help the team already under siege, or they were just arriving to begin their shift, the shooters couldn't have much grasp of who or what they were confronting. Any hesitancy on their part could only work in Bolan's favor, but the window of opportunity wouldn't stay open for long. Learning that only one man stood against them, they would be emboldened and determined to eliminate him.

And they just might pull it off.

He heard them coming now, feet double-timing on concrete, just past the point where he had taken down two of their cohorts with a frag grenade. The bloody tableau hadn't stopped them, much less turned them back. A few more yards and Bolan would be facing them, with no place for anyone on either side to hide.

But then the sounds of footsteps paused. A voice called out to him—to someone, anyway—asking, *"Quem é você? O que você quer?"*

He took a chance, calling back. "Try English."

After momentary hesitation, the commanding voice replied, "Who are you? What do you want?"

Easing his last grenade out of a pocket, Bolan couldn't think of any reason not to answer honestly. "I'm taking down the plant," he said. "I'm taking down your Family."

Another hesitation then, before the voice asked, "You are not police?"

He pulled the pin but held the arming spoon in place as he replied, "Not even close."

Arm back, ready to make the pitch, he heard the disembodied voice ask, "Were you sent by General Sanhá? By Admiral Pires?"

"You're getting cold," he said, while edging forward, nearly close enough to make another bank shot with the frag grenade.

Bolan nearly pitched it when the firing started, but he quickly realized the ripping slugs weren't aimed his way. Short bursts of automatic fire sounded like 9 mm Parabellum rounds, and garbled cries came from the men receiving them. It lasted six or seven seconds, then the corridor was silent but for muffled voices from the cutting room behind him.

Then a voice in front told the Executioner, "The rest are dead. May I approach you?"

Frowning, Bolan thought about it. If it was a trick…

"Slowly," he said, still clutching the grenade, his rifle's folding stock braced tight against his hip for single-handed firing. "You're covered all the way."

He heard the shooter's footsteps edging around obstacles before a slender man stepped into view. He stood five nine or ten and might have weighed 160 pounds. A submachine gun dangled from his right hand, smoking muzzle pointed toward the floor. He studied Bolan for a moment, checking out his weapons, then looked past him toward the cutting room.

"You have unfinished business," he observed.

"I'm taking one thing at a time," Bolan replied.

"Of course. Perhaps the pin for that grenade?"

"It's safe, for now," Bolan assured him. "You are?"

"Nilson Medina," the shooter replied. "On assignment with the Judicial Police."

4

Cupelon de Cima, Bissau

Edouard Camara didn't appreciate bad news. His second glass of Agwa de Bolivia liqueur, distilled from coca leaves, helped moderate his temper, but he felt rage simmering behind his sternum like a savage bout of heartburn, anxious to explode.

"Explain how this could happen," he demanded of the messenger, his second in command.

"I only know what I have told you," Aristide Ialá replied, his tone cautiously neutral. "It appears that one man was responsible."

"One man," Camara repeated. "Against…what was it? A dozen?"

"That's right. Except that one of them is missing now."

"One missing, and eleven dead," Camara said and sipped his drink.

Ialá nodded silently.

"And so," Camara pressed, "we know it was a single man because…?"

"The cutters," Ialá replied.

"Of course. They described him?"

"A white man. Beyond that, not much. They were frightened, and after he blew up the merchandise, well…"

Camara had another thought. "This missing man. Do you suppose that he was taken hostage?"

"It's unclear. As to the killings, there are some…discrepancies."

"Explain."

"The shift on duty when the fighting started—Bruno and his men—were mostly shot with an assault rifle, two of them killed by a grenade. But the relief crew, with Fidelis…"

"What?" Camara demanded.

"It appears they were shot in the back, with a different weapon," Ialá explained.

"And you know this because?"

"I'm informed by the Special Intervention Police"

Camara sometimes thought of the SIP as *his* police force, though it answered to General Diallo.

"Two weapons means two shooters, eh?" he said. "The cutters must have been mistaken."

"Or the missing man could be a traitor," Ialá said.

"What's his name?"

"Nilson Medina. He came highly recommended. Blooded prior to his recruitment, with a record."

"Which was verified?"

"As usual, sir. Through channels with the Judicial Police," Ialá said.

"If we can trust them," Camara replied.

"You believe they'd risk an agent undercover, with so few on staff?"

"We won't know till we find and question this Medina, will we, Aristide?"

"If he is still alive."

"And if he's not, it solves our problem," Camara said. "On the other hand, if he *is* breathing, then he has become a liability. Either a traitor or a hostage who can tell his captors everything he knows about our Family. In either case—"

"We'll find him," Ialá stated. "I already have men searching for him."

"Excellent," Camara said. "As for the white man, how hard can it be to find him in Bissau? Whether he's British, French or Portuguese, he'll have been seen."

"And if he is American?" Ialá asked.

"No difference. Find him. Bring him to me alive, if possible. Wherever he is from, we need to know if he was sent on some official project, or if he's a mercenary. And if so, who paid him to attack us."

"It must be Admiral Pires or General Sanhá," Ialá said. "Who else would dare to challenge General Diallo?"

"That's the question we must answer, Aristide. And soon."

Camara had already thought of other possibilities. An outside syndicate—perhaps Italian, Corsican or even Russian—might feel threatened by the flow of drugs from Guinea-Bissau into Europe. All were ruthless, capable of reaching out to strike their adversaries from a distance. And if war was brewing on an intercontinental scale, Camara had to know before his patron learned of it at army headquarters.

Before it came around to bite him on the ass when he least expected it.

Calequir, Bissau

THE SAFE HOUSE was a small two-bedroom dwelling in a neighborhood of winding narrow streets between Estrada da Granja do Pessube and Estrada de Santa Luzia, north of downtown Bissau. It was dark when Bolan reached it, his passenger navigating from the shotgun seat. At Medina's direction, he followed an unpaved driveway to a mangy yard of sorts behind the house, then turned the Peugeot 308 around so that it stood facing the street for a speedy departure at need.

The house was dark, as was the neighborhood surrounding it. Bolan decided he would take his rifle with him, leaving his RPG-7 and rockets locked up in the trunk. If something happened and he needed high explosives to escape the house, he would rely on the grenades clipped to his belt beneath his windbreaker.

Nilson Medina had explained himself after a fashion, while directing Bolan to his hideaway. At thirty-three, he was a ten-year veteran of the Judicial Police, assigned to infiltrate Edouard Camara's drug syndicate in the guise of a felon with nothing to lose, seeking profit wherever a dishonest CFA franc could be made. He'd been accepted to the Family, kept filing his reports with headquarters, but nothing ever seemed to happen. Recently, one of his fellow officers had been assassinated, almost certainly by other cops—the Special Intervention Force—and he was getting fed up with his job.

"Still," Bolan had observed, "you took a chance tonight. You're on the hook for murder now."

Medina shrugged at that and said, "What difference does it make? I stopped a crime in progress. If I'm prosecuted and convicted, they will send me to First Squadron and I'll walk away. It's all a joke, you see."

"Not for the boys you put away tonight," Bolan reminded him. "Camara will have people looking for you now."

Medina hadn't answered that, but now, inside his safe house with doors locked against the hostile night and coffee on the kitchen table, he told Bolan, "I was getting nowhere with the system as it is. We can collect intelligence from now until the end of time, but to what end? No one dares move against the men behind the trafficking in drugs—or children, for that matter. Did you know that girls as young as eight and nine years old are sold in Senegal? For service as domestics, we are told, but who can say?"

"I didn't know it, but I'm not surprised," Bolan replied. Trafficking in children was a global scandal, whether they wound up with pedophiles or slaving in some filthy sweatshop for pennies a day. Bolan had dealt with human traffickers before, but it was like declaring war on cockroaches. No matter how many went down, more always stood in line to take their place.

"It's foolish, I suppose," Medina said, "but when I heard your voice tonight I had to *do* something. Fidelis and the others would have killed you, held a celebration, and the world would just have gone on as before."

In fact, Bolan was more concerned about the prospect that he might have killed an undercover cop and never known it, but he didn't contradict Medina. Why puncture his illusion, when the guy had risked his life for Bolan, possibly destroying his career?

Instead, he told his host, "Well, I appreciate your help. What now?"

"I think we have an opportunity," Medina said, "to break the Family. Perhaps we cannot touch General Diallo, but Camara may be vulnerable."

"You and me," Bolan said.

"Yes." Medina nodded earnestly.

"You understand I'm not a cop. I don't have a book of rules. We wouldn't be collecting evidence or bringing anyone to trial."

"That's all a waste of time, in any case," Medina said. "Our president dismisses judges on a whim, replacing them with cronies who support him, then ignores complaints from the United Nations. Even if the courts were independent and relieved of all corruption, who would try the men behind Camara and his kind? Oppose the generals, and you invite another coup."

"Just so you're ready for whatever happens next," warned Bolan.

"I am ready," Medina said with a smile. "When do we start?"

Headquarters of the Forces Armées de Guinée-Bissau, Bairro Militar, Bissau

"AND WHY IS THIS MY PROBLEM?" General Ismael Diallo asked his unexpected visitor.

Edouard Camara frowned, as if he didn't fully understand the question, then replied, "Because, General, the plant was your facility as well as mine."

"Was it?" Diallo asked, frowning. "If that is true, I should be angry that you failed to keep it safe. Do you present yourself for punishment?"

Camara shifted in his chair, doubly uneasy now. "I meant to say—"

"By all means, tell me what you *meant* to say," Diallo interrupted him. "It's late, and I'm expected elsewhere."

"There is a possibility—no, say a *probability*—that the attack was planned, commissioned if you like, by forces from outside the country. Clearly, that is your field of authority and expertise."

"What would you have me do?" Diallo asked. "Should I ask the foreign consulates in Bissau if they are responsible? Perhaps you'd have me call Dakar and question the Americans? They would be pleased to answer truthfully, I'm sure."

"General, I simply mean that when the culprit is identified—"

"Aha!" Diallo wore a predatory smile. "And that's the problem, is it not, Edouard? The culprit, as you call him, *has not* been identified. You say he was a white man. So, what of it? That narrows the field to Europe, North America, Australia— am I overlooking any possibilities?"

"I doubt that the Australians—"

"Russians, then? The *vor v zakone?* Perhaps it was the Mafia or Unione Corse? Is there a possibility your addled witnesses mistook a Mexican or a Colombian for white?"

"General, the man spoke English."

"Yes, according to your soldier who lay dying."

"I would trust him all the more for that," Camara said.

"Then follow up on that," Diallo said. "You know what steps to take. Contact the airport for recent arrivals. Check the hotels. Use your eyes and ears inside the Judicial Police."

"I shall," Camara said. "As to the airport, General, your own men might have more success with Customs than my own."

Diallo considered that for a moment, then nodded. "I'll send someone from Special Intervention," he agreed. "Now, if that's all…"

Camara clearly wasn't satisfied, but he knew when to quit. "Yes, General," he said. "Your help is much appreciated."

"You'd be wise to clean this up, Edouard," Diallo warned the gangster as he rose to leave. "It would be most unfortunate if you appeared to be incapable of dealing with a crisis. I would have to wonder if you were…expendable."

"I'll see to it, General," Camara said, and scuttled out before Diallo had a chance to change his mind.

Calequir, Bissau

NILSON MEDINA STIRRED the pot of stew that bubbled on his stove and wondered whether he had lost his mind. The tall American he knew as Matthew Cooper—an alias perhaps, but it didn't matter—sat nearby, checking a list of targets that Medina had compiled against a city map of Bissau. Charting their approach, presumably, and paths for their escape.

Madness.

And yet, he didn't feel as if he'd gone insane. Quite the reverse, in fact. Medina felt as if his long months working undercover in Edouard Camara's crime family had been a waste of time and energy that verged on masochistic self-abuse. Each day he'd witnessed crimes that would have sent his targets off to prison in a normal country, with police and courts working together for the public good. Sometimes he'd been forced to swallow hysterical laughter, realizing that nothing he saw or reported would take even one monster off the streets.

Ironically, the muffled laughter at odd times had helped his cover, made the psychopaths he worked with daily think Medina had to be one of them—or maybe even worse. He'd kept up the charade, knowing that it was useless, until he'd been forced to make a choice that night.

Now, in the law's eyes, he would be a murderer. As if that mattered in Bissau. Police might shoot a killer if they caught him in the act, but otherwise, what punishment was there? Not execution, which had been abolished by the parliament. Perhaps consignment to First Squadron, where he'd wait a night or two before he wriggled out a window, crawled out through an open sewer line or simply strolled past sleeping guards to freedom in the moonlight.

So, he'd made a snap decision in the heat of battle, which had paired him with a foreigner embarking on what sounded like a suicidal quest. To what end?

Would the stew he'd offered to prepare before they set out into darkness be his final meal?

And did it even matter?

Medina had no family to speak of—none he kept in touch with, anyway. No lover, wife or children. Not even a cat to mourn him if he never made it back to his small flat in Santa Luzia, northeast of the city center. His landlord would wonder where he'd gone—or where his monthly check had gone, at least—and would throw out Medina's things after a week or so, perhaps after inquiring at the Ministry of Justice headquarters.

So be it.

Medina wasn't suicidal, wasn't even tired of living, but he felt his life so far had largely been a waste. He had joined the Judicial Police with a hope of improving his country, or at least life in its capital. Perhaps he'd been naive, or even foolish. He'd accomplished nothing so far, aside from consoling occasional victims of crime. To what end, when he couldn't protect them or promise them justice?

The American, Medina thought, might be his last hope for… for *what?* A gesture or statement of some kind, before he was swept from the world and forgotten?

Perhaps.

Or they might accomplish something greater, root out certain characters who helped make life in Guinea-Bissau a depressing daily hell on earth. Something to shoot for, at the very least. And shooting there would be. He had no doubt of that.

"The stew is ready," he announced, tipping it from the pot into a pair of mismatched bowls. *"Bom apetite!"*

Bairro Militar, Bissau

PASCAL KINTE HAD BALKED at meeting General Diallo inside army headquarters. Some people who had stepped inside that edifice were never seen again, and while the nation's Minister of the Interior felt reasonably safe, he also bore in mind that soldiers had deposed three presidents of Guinea-Bissau, killing one of them, within as many decades.

Even after granting Kinte's request for a meeting on neutral ground, Diallo had refused to leave the Military District, west of downtown Bissau. As a compromise, they were meeting at one of a half dozen officers' clubs in the neighborhood, this one catering to members of the army. The management wouldn't expel a ranking officer from the air force or navy, but either one would find the atmosphere inside the club unwelcoming, to say the least. Such rivalries were common, Kinte understood—and all the more so in a nation where the several branches of its military service were, in effect, competing criminal syndicates.

As a civilian, albeit among the highest office holders in the land, Kinte felt like the odd man out as he entered the club—called Diamonds—shortly after nine o'clock. The club was fairly crowded, and approximately half of the male patrons wore some variation of their daily uniforms. Many wore sidearms, Kinte saw, and he wondered if he should have brought along the bodyguard who normally escorted him to meetings in the daytime.

Too late now. It would be cowardly of him to turn around and leave. Aside from angering the general, it would reveal a weakness that inevitably would destabilize their partnership.

A hostess was approaching Kinte when he saw Diallo seated in a booth, off to his left. He waved the young woman away and went to join the general, sliding into the booth without first asking for permission to sit down. It was a petty thing, perhaps, but still asserted independence of a sort.

Diallo skipped the normal salutation, saying, "I suppose you've heard by now."

"About the shooting? Yes." Kinte avoided any mention of the factory per se, or of its function for the syndicate.

"It cost us something like 230 million francs," Diallo said.

Kinte performed the calculation in his head. Say half a million U.S. dollars, or 437,000 Swiss francs on exchange at his bank in Zurich. As an afterthought, he added, "And the men who died."

Diallo waved that thought away. "They were Camara's," he replied. "Street thugs. There is no shortage of them in Bissau."

"What has been done to punish those responsible?" Kinte inquired.

"Edouard has orders to locate them," Diallo said, without stating that the orders came from him. That much was understood between them. "And the Special Intervention Force will help, as necessary."

"So, it's handled, then," Kinte stated.

"I believe so," the general replied. "But there is one discrepancy."

"Namely?"

"A missing man. One of Camara's pawns, supposedly."

"You doubt it?" Kinte asked.

"I don't like leaving anything to chance," Diallo said.

Kinte nodded and asked the question he'd been dreading. "How may I assist you, General?"

"Use your resources to discover whether he, this missing one, is what he claimed to be or…something else."

"The name?" Kinte inquired.

"Nilson Medina. Or, at least, that's what he called himself."

A relatively simple task, Kinte thought. It shouldn't be dangerous.

"I'll see what I can find," he said, "and let you know."

"Sooner rather than later," the general told him. "We have no time to waste."

Ministry of Justice, Estrada da Granja do Passube, Bissau

JOSEPH MANSARÉ WAS WORRIED. Hours had passed since the shootings at Edouard Camara's drug-cutting plant, and now one of Mansaré's men was missing in the aftermath of mayhem. As a captain of the Judicial Police, with fewer than seventy officers still on the job nationwide, he couldn't afford to lose another.

Particularly not Nilson Medina.

Months ago, Medina had gone undercover with Camara's syndicate, filing reports religiously on each new violation of the law that he observed firsthand. Captain Mansaré had been filing those reports, collecting them, in hopes that someday soon reform would overtake the capital, perhaps encouraged by persistent pressure from United Nations headquarters, permitting prosecution of the drug lords who had turned Guinea-Bissau into a global laughingstock.

Of course, Mansaré knew what that could mean for Bissau and the country as a whole. His memories of military uprisings were fresh and vivid. There was every chance, he thought, that three or four top-ranking officers would balk at being taken into custody and tried for crimes that might mean life in prison. If the country *had* a prison worthy of the name. Only the threat of intervention from outside could possibly restrain them from unleashing hell upon the feeble justice system— and, perhaps, upon each other—in defense of what was truly, now, a narco state.

But what form would the outside intervention take, assuming that it ever came? Would it be of the lazy watch-and-wait variety that had already failed so monumentally in Rwanda and Sudan? Or would the lightning strike efficiently, as was the case in Libya? That had been NATO's operation, sanctioned by the UN, but the North Atlantic Treaty Organization had no visible interest in sub-Saharan Africa. The Organization of African Unity might have been helpful, but it had disbanded in 2002.

No, Mansaré thought, they were alone. And even worse, divided by internal rifts that might be insurmountable. The Special Intervention Force, controlled by General Diallo and his army cohorts, was ostensibly a law enforcement agency but sometimes operated as a military hit team for Camara's syndicate. Assassination of General Batista Tagme Na Waie in 2009 had removed the country's last military chief of staff, leaving the army, air force and navy to operate as de facto independent bodies. Thus far, neither the air force nor the navy matched Diallo's strength in manpower, although Mansaré thought a three-way war between the military branches might succeed in wiping Guinea-Bissau off the map.

And now, his only man inside the army-dominated syndicate had disappeared. Mansaré didn't know if Medina was dead, had been taken captive by someone or if he was simply in hiding after the factory massacre. Unless he reached out soon, Mansaré reckoned he would have to start from scratch and risk another agent's life.

For what? The captain scowled, thinking, *for justice.*

But the bitter churning in his stomach told him it might be a futile exercise.

5

Chão de Papel, Bissau

"This way," Nilson Medina said, directing Bolan to turn left and leave Estrada de Bandim, eastbound. "Two blocks, perhaps a little less."

Bolan followed directions, watching out for headlights in his rearview mirror, even as he scanned the street ahead of him for any sign of a potential ambush. They were passing homes and shops, mixed in together without seeming rhyme or reason, looking for the address Medina had placed at the top of their hit list for Bissau.

An arms cache, hidden from police—if any had been looking for it—at a haulage company called *Transporte Tempestade,* or Storm Transport in English. Bolan wasn't sure if someone had a pun in mind when they had named the company; in fact, he didn't care much, either way. Hitting Camara's arsenal would send a message, maybe leave his troops short of matériel, and maybe net some hardware on the side for Bolan and his unexpected ally.

"There," Medina told him, pointing, just as Bolan saw the parking lot surrounded by an eight-foot chain-link fence with razor wire on top. Inside the fence sat half a dozen trucks of varied makes and sizes. Bolan saw two Nissan Diesels, one Dongfeng, a BMC from Turkey, a Mahindra Navistar from India and a Tata Daewoo made in South Korea. Guinea-Bissau manufac-

tured no vehicles of its own, at any size or price, which kept the
money badly needed on the home front flowing out of country.

Bolan drove around Storm Transport on surrounding access roads and found no point of entry other than the wide
front gate, which was secured with chain and padlock. There
were no signs to suggest the chain-link fence had been electrified or otherwise equipped with security devices beyond the
wicked coils of razor wire on top. Two floodlights bathed the
trucks out front with bright illumination, but the yard in back
was dark. Bolan slowed and let Medina whistle at the fence,
but no dogs surfaced in response.

"They had none on the property the last time I was here,"
Medina said.

"And it's just left unguarded overnight?" Bolan asked, skeptical.

Medina shrugged. "The weapons are supposed to be a secret. Anyone who'd know about them also knows who they
belong to. If Camara's reputation does not keep them out, the
fear of General Diallo will."

All clear, then, if Medina had the straight of it. And if he
didn't?

Bolan had no thought of the policeman leading him into a
trap. It would have been bizarre beyond belief, an undercover
cop blowing his mission, killing half a dozen mobsters, just
to snare a stranger he couldn't have known existed prior to
the event. That *didn't* mean Medina was correct about the lot
being unguarded, though. Caution would be required to get
them past the fence and back again.

Beginning now.

Bolan parked at the southeast corner of the fence, switching
off the Peugeot's dome light as the engine died. There were no
homes within a clear line of sight, but why take chances with
a sudden glare of light? Both dressed in black, they stood beside the car and double-checked their weapons, leaving safeties
off, rounds in the chambers as a hedge against surprise. Medina drew a pair of wire cutters from one of his pants pockets,

crouched beside the chain-link near the car and went to work, while Bolan stood watch over him.

No dogs, no guards, no sudden flare of spotlights in the night. Three minutes saw Medina finished, peeling back a flap of fencing large enough for one of them to enter at a time, on hands and knees. The African went first, then held the flap for Bolan. After both of them were clear, he put it back in place and used a simple twist-tie to secure it against casual inspection in the dark.

Easy, so far.

Bolan still half expected an alarm as they approached the combination office and garage, despite Medina's confident assurance that there would be none. "Who would respond?" he'd asked, while they were driving over.

The soldier couldn't say, but he'd be checking out the door and windows carefully, before he tried to breach their locks. There was no good excuse for being careless now, when it could blow up in his face and get them killed.

THERE WAS, IN FACT, a guard on duty at Storm Transport, though he missed the hostile penetration of the firm's perimeter. Malam Furtado was distracted by a porn website that he'd bookmarked on the laptop he had stolen from a schoolchild on the street, several months earlier. The theft hadn't troubled Furtado's conscience, possibly because he had none, but he justified it on the grounds that thousands of cheap computers, costing only $150 apiece, had been distributed throughout West Africa by an American philanthropist, under the banner of One Laptop Per Child.

Who was this foreigner, undoubtedly a white man, who was hell-bent on corrupting African youth with free internet porn? That was a privilege reserved for certified adults. In fact, Furtado managed to convince himself that he had *saved* the boy he robbed from degradation by the very Asian sluts who now performed before Furtado's eyes.

He was a hero, in his own way!

But not a watchman worthy of his paycheck, it turned out.

He only knew that there were prowlers on the property when he experienced a server hang-up and was suddenly aware of voices in the night, outside the building where he sat in darkness, feet up on a corner of the company manager's desk, waiting for his access to the information superhighway to resume.

Prowlers?

They likely intended to steal one of the trucks, or maybe all of them. Furtado wasn't in the loop concerning any contraband concealed around the premises. It never crossed his mind, although his thoughts flashed to the three marijuana cigarettes he carried in a pocket of his shirt. If he went out and caught the would-be thieves, his next step would be summoning police. What if they searched him for some reason? It didn't seem likely, but without a guarantee...

Quickly, he hid the three joints in a top drawer of the desk, then rose and drew his pistol. It wasn't a new one, or expensive, just a 9 mm Llama made in Spain before the company went bankrupt in the early 1990s. It would kill, all right, if Furtado could aim it correctly—a big *if,* that one, since he'd only fired the pistol twice during the four years since he bought it off the street.

He knew enough to rack the weapon's slide, putting a live round in the chamber, and he left the safety off, his index finger well outside the trigger guard for now. Furtado remembered the sound and recoil of the pistol from last time, a bungled attempt at rat hunting some eighteen months earlier. But could he use it on a man?

Perhaps. If he felt threatened, definitely.

In a flash, while he was moving from the desk chair toward the exit, Furtado saw himself on television, being interviewed about the robbery he'd foiled. The men who ran Storm Transport would be thrilled, of course. They might even—

No, wait!

If he appeared on television, it was likely he'd be seen by the first owner of his laptop. What would happen when the boy described their brief encounter on the street? All things considered, Furtado would probably lose his job if he was known for robbing children. Maybe he should just stay where he was and…what?

Let thieves steal all the trucks? He *definitely* would be fired in that case, maybe even beaten by the rough types he had seen around the place. And what if the prowlers came into the building, looking for money? Should he hide in the closet like a coward until they had looted the place and gone on their way?

Angry at himself now for being so frightened, Furtado moved toward the door on trembling legs, silently cursing his bad luck.

NILSON MEDINA FELT strangely relaxed. It was peculiar, he realized, when he should have been worried about so many things: his execution of six gangsters, the probable loss of his job, his involvement with the grim American in an illegal campaign that would most likely get him killed. Yet none of that fazed him just now, as they moved through darkness toward the back door of the building where he knew a cache of arms and ammunition was concealed.

They were Edouard Camara's weapons, held in reserve for his soldiers, as if support from General Diallo and the army was inadequate to make Camara feel secure.

Of course, the general couldn't ask regular troops to fight his battles on the streets of Bissau. On occasion, members of the Special Intervention Force might help, but Diallo preferred that Camara solve his own problems whenever possible, leaving the great man in peace with his profits. Destroying the stockpile would hurt Camara as much as the loss of his cocaine at the cutting plant, or more so, since the weapons would take longer to replace.

The back door to the shop was double-locked, with a keyhole in the doorknob and a separate deadbolt. Instead of trying to finagle them, Matt Cooper produced a pistol with a sound suppressor appended to its muzzle, warned Medina to stand back and fired a muffled shot into the doorknob, blowing it away. Two shots were needed for the deadbolt, punching it back into space where it clattered on concrete.

Still holding the pistol ready, Cooper hooked two fingers of his left hand through the hole left by the deadbolt and pulled the door open. The room beyond the threshold was a dark cave, but faint light was visible beyond it, coming through another door that stood ajar.

Medina followed Cooper inside, holding his Spectre submachine gun with its muzzle pointed toward the floor. Its double-action trigger let him keep a live round in the weapon's chamber with the safety off, ready to fire at any moment. Its 50-round quad-column casket magazine was fully loaded, with the fire selector set for 3-round bursts. Not that he needed all that firepower to raid an empty building.

Still…

"Which way?" Cooper asked him, pausing at the partly open door.

"Through there and to your left," Medina said. "In the garage they have three service pits, but only two are used for trucks. The third one, farthest from the door as you go in, is covered by a steel plate. Underneath, they keep the guns, with ammunition and explosives, all together. There was Semtex last time I was here. Tonight, who knows?"

"Let's find out," Cooper replied, and led the way along a short hall to the truck garage.

The light they'd seen on entering had come from there, a single bulb over a workbench set against the spacious room's west wall. Medina didn't know if it was left on by mistake, or as a matter of routine, since he had never visited the place at night before. It was convenient, either way, guiding them past welding equipment and machines used for repairing tires, an air compressor and a tool cabinet on wheels. Without the light, Medina thought, the shop would have become a bruising maze.

They stood over the farthest service pit, Cooper studying the slab of metal capping it. Steel rings were set into the plate at either end, to aid in lifting it aside. Medina guessed that it had to weigh a hundred pounds or more, but he thought they could handle it, between the two of them.

"Ready?" Cooper asked.

Medina nodded. "Yes. Ready."

"You take the other end. We'll slide this over and see what they left for us."

Medina walked down to the far end of the pit, and set his weapon in the concrete floor. Stooping, he clutched the metal rings, prepared to lift on his companion's command and haul the metal plate aside.

"On three," Cooper said. "One…"

"Pare!" a shaky voice said from behind Medina. *"Estabelecer suas armas! Levantem as mãos!"*

Medina translated for Cooper without turning to face the stranger. "He demands that we lay down our guns and raise our hands."

"No guard, eh?" Cooper said.

"It seems I was mistaken," Medina replied. "If we live, I hope you will accept my most sincere apology."

MALAM FURTADO HEARD the prowlers speaking English and was even more unnerved than when he'd first confirmed their presence in the building. Finding them armed with automatic weapons was another shock, his old pistol suddenly inadequate. One of the pair spoke Portuguese, at least, and was translating for the other, as it seemed, although Furtado wasn't sure.

A moment passed, then both placed their machine guns on the concrete floor. Furtado edged into the room with nervous baby steps, his Llama sweeping back and forth to cover one man, then the other. They were far enough apart that watching both of them was difficult. If they leaped off in opposite directions, a coordinated movement, which should he shoot first? Or *try* to, since he had no confidence in hitting either.

Making up his mind, Furtado told the African, *"Se aproximam mais!"* The black man said something in English and the two of them obeyed his order, edging closer together.

Was that a mistake? Furtado couldn't say. He wasn't a policeman or tactician, just a lowly security guard paid by the hour to keep burglars out. No one had ever briefed him on what he should do if he caught one *inside*. In fact, he had only one standing order: if anything happened requiring attention, Furtado was to call his boss, not the police.

That might have seemed suspicious in some other country, but in Guinea-Bissau it was more or less routine. Police were spread so thin, and they were so inept, that calling them to handle an emergency was like a form of gambling. Would they come at all? And if so, would they help or make things worse?

Furtado's mind snapped back to his two prisoners. What now?

He had no handcuffs, and wouldn't have dared to approach them, regardless. Cuffing one, or binding him in any way, meant laying down the Llama pistol. And without the gun, Furtado sensed, he was as good as dead.

All right. He had to contain them while he placed the call to his employer, then sit back and keep them covered until help arrived. That shouldn't be too difficult. There was a telephone in the garage, on the south wall. Furtado saw no reason why he couldn't hold his gun in one hand, dialing with the other, and have reinforcements on the scene in…what? Say half an hour, at the most?

"Stay where you are," he told the black intruder, leaving him to translate for the white man, but instead, the African replied, "You don't work for Camara, do you?"

"Who?" Furtado asked reflexively, regretting it almost before the word had left his lips.

"Edouard Camara," the prowler replied. "I suspect you recognize the name."

Of course Furtado did. Camara was notorious and filthy rich. Why would this prowler think Camara was involved with Storm Transport?

Against his better judgment, Furtado said, "I work for Capital Security and watch this place six nights a week. Edouard Camara, no."

"But you *are* working for him, brother," the burglar said. "We have come to here to destroy the weapons he keeps hidden in this pit."

Weapons? Why would a trucking company need weapons,

other than for self-defense? Still, it *was* odd, two armed invaders seeking access to a service pit in the garage, instead of stealing trucks or seeking money from the office. Then again, if Storm Transport had weapons in the pit, what business was it of Furtado's? He was paid to guard the premises and all that it contained from 6:00 p.m. to 6:00 a.m., Monday through Saturday.

"You're stealing," he replied. "That's all I know. Stand still. I need to make a call."

But as he half turned toward the telephone, the white man moved so suddenly that there was no time to react. A gun was in his hand like magic, and it made a muffled chugging sound, before a double hammer stroke to his chest propelled Furtado into contact with the nearest work bench. Gasping, suddenly unable to draw breath, he toppled to the floor, unconscious.

"THAT'S MOST UNFORTUNATE," Medina said.

"Agreed. But we couldn't let him make that call. Hopefully he won't die from blood loss before someone finds him. We'll move him to the yard on the way out."

Medina nodded, then came back to help him shift the heavy cover from the service pit. Inside, revealed in half light from the single bulb above the work bench, wooden crates were stacked by size. Some were long enough for rifles, others squat and square, presumably containing ammunition, magazines or the Semtex Medina had referred to earlier.

"Let's have a look," Bolan suggested, then descended via metal stairs that occupied one corner of the pit. A pry bar lay atop one of the larger crates, and Bolan quickly had its lid off, baring half a dozen AK-47s to the light, well oiled and packed in straw.

"Bingo," he said, and moved on to a smaller crate. Grenades in that one, Semtex in the top crate of the stack beside it.

"What we need," he told Medina, "are the detonators."

Storing detonators with explosives is the biggest no-no in the arms trade, nearly any novice being smart enough to figure out that placing them in close proximity to each other was an invitation to disaster—and to sudden death. Bolan still checked the pit, but came up empty. While Medina went to check the nearby cabinets, before heading to the other rooms, Bolan proceeded to collect supplies he thought might prove useful in their campaign.

Some of the Semtex, for a start, would be a bonus, then two cases of 9 mm Parabellum ammunition and one of 7.62 mm NATO rounds. He had them stacked up on the floor above the service pit when Medina called out, "Here they are!"

He brought a box of blasting caps back from a cabinet on the west wall of the garage. "The box says fuses," he explained. "If no one looked inside, they would suppose fuses for trucks."

"Not even close," Bolan replied, viewing the detonators wrapped in layers of cotton. "Now we need some kind of timer."

"I'll go look," Medina said, and went to search the building's other rooms. Bolan descended to the pit once more, removed the yellow blocks of Semtex from their crate and started planting them among the stacks of wooden boxes holding guns and ammunition. By the time he'd placed a detonator in each charge, Medina had returned, lugging a microwave oven.

"This has a timer," he said. "It is all I could find. But as to the wiring…" He shrugged.

"We can manage," Bolan told him. "Plug it in as close as possible, then help me find some wire for the connections."

Fifteen minutes later, they had rigged an octopus of slender wires attached to half a dozen detonators and were ready to depart. One trip removed the cases they were keeping to the back steps, after which Bolan knelt to set the microwave's timer for twenty minutes. More than time enough for them to clear the lot, the fence, the neighborhood.

They had dropped Furtado in a safe place, pressed combat dressings to his wounds and were a quarter-mile away when Storm Transport ceased to exist, consumed by flame and thunder, sending out a shock wave that cracked windows in a four-block radius. Bolan imagined ammunition cooking off in the inferno, sounding like a war zone.

Which, in fact, it was.

The Executioner had brought his war to Guinea-Bissau with a vengeance, no holds barred.

And he was blitzing on.

6

Hal Brognola was relaxing at home with a glass of whiskey when the phone rang on his desk. He recognized the muted grumble of his private line at once and frowned. It rarely brought good news, and even then it nearly always meant that someone had been killed.

He set down his glass and reached for the phone, hoping the right people would be dead.

"Hello," he said. The scrambler kicked in automatically, defeating any eavesdroppers.

"I'm just updating," Bolan said without preamble or a salutation, speaking to him from tomorrow and forty-two hundred miles eastward. "We're up two to nothing and counting."

"Did I hear you say *we?*" Brognola inquired, with a frown. "Does that mean us?"

"Funny thing," Bolan said. "At the first stop, a cop under cover came out of the closet to help."

"That's a fluke," Brognola replied. "He's legit? Is it *he?*"

"Yes and yes," Bolan answered. "I saw his ID. Seems he's burned out on swimming upstream, getting nowhere."

"Your call," the big Fed allowed, "but it sounds like a bad career move."

"I suggested a contact. He's thinking it over. I'll leave it with him."

"Which department?" Brognola asked.

"The Judicial Police."

"And you figure he's clean?"

"If he's not," Bolan answered, "the people who bought him are going to be disappointed."

"As long as he doesn't sell you down the river."

"I'm on top of it," Bolan assured him. "No contact with regulars yet, but Camara's guys know someone's working their turf."

"About those regulars," Brognola said, "you need to keep an eye out for the Special Intervention Force. They're cops, at least on paper, but—"

"I know. And I'm playing by the rules."

"*Your* rules," the big Fed answered back.

"That's right."

Brognola recognized Bolan's commitment to abstain from cop-killing, regardless of the circumstances, and while he appreciated that stand as a former G-man, he could also say that there were so-called lawmen he'd have dropped the hammer on in nothing flat, if it came down to life-or-death time. Take those two in New York City, for example, who had served as hit men for the Mafia. Or the six who'd been arrested back in 2010, for taking out the mayor of Santiago, Mexico. Hell, Mexico's entire Federal Judicial Police force had been disbanded in 2002, for corruption, replaced by a new Federal Investigations Agency—and *that* outfit had only lasted seven years before it had to be dismantled.

Bottom line: Brognola had been a cop of one kind or another most of his adult life, and he knew damn well from personal experience that some of his brothers behind the badge—"soldiers of the same side" in Bolan's parlance—deserved no more than a solitary cell or a swift lethal injection. Still, if the Executioner exempted cops en masse from his attentions, there was nothing the big Fed could do to change his mind.

"You'll watch it, though?" he asked, hoping it didn't sound like nagging to his oldest living friend.

"You know I will," Bolan replied.

"Okay, then. If there's anything you need…"

"I'll let you know."

"Right. Stay frosty, guy."

"West Africa," Bolan said. "Frost is hard to come by. Later."

And the line went dead. No lingering over goodbyes, and what would be the point, when any might be the last?

Brognola didn't see himself as fatalistic, though he tended to be cynical. What lawman wasn't, if he'd spent more than a weekend on the job? You went in hoping to be good, to make a difference, and wound up satisfied if you went home alive, in one piece, when your shift was over. As for "saving" anyone, what did that even mean today?

Helping the relatively innocent to stay alive, perhaps, if only for another day or two.

Before the next damned predator showed up.

"God keep," he told the silent room, and reached for his whiskey.

Cupelon de Cima, Bissau

"Yes, I understand," Edouard Camara said. "There were no witnesses? Yes, thank you, you'll receive the normal bonus."

After he cut the link, Camara wondered why in hell he was thanking the policeman who had called. For bringing more bad news? He'd lost more valuable property, and this attack would do more damage to his reputation than the first, if left unpunished. But who *could* he punish to set an example, with no ID for the person or persons behind the assaults?

Camara understood the motive—first to weaken, then destroy him—but that didn't help identify his enemy. There were too many of them for a random guess to do much good. He thought at once of Amilcar Mané and Danilson Pinhel, his main competitors, but would the navy or the air force back their leading traffickers in what amounted to a war against the army under General Diallo?

Doubtful.

Then, he had the vague description of a white man from the first attack, whatever that might mean. Since Guinea-Bissau had become the leading hub for cocaine shipments from West Africa to Europe, more white "tourists" had been visiting the capital. Nearly all of them were male, well dressed, with faces that betrayed hard lives. Camara had been visited by Brits and Irishmen, by French and Dutch importers, by crude Russians and one elderly Sicilian who complained about the weather and the food while bargaining for drugs.

Any or all of them might move against Camara if they thought removing him would grant them some advantage. Each had doubtless ordered death for dozens, maybe hundreds, in their respective homelands, but Camara thought they were probably wise enough to avoid direct confrontation with General Diallo in a nation as unstable as Guinea-Bissau. To remove Camara personally, hoping his successor might negotiate a lower price per kilo, would be one thing. But an all-out war against his Family was something else. Why not simply go shopping from the other military services instead?

And there was still the problem of his missing soldier from the first attack. The name Nilsen Medina meant no more to him than that of any other peasant on the street, but he had passed inspection for recruitment by the Family, a proven killer with a record of arrests, albeit futile ones. For him to vanish, leaving six dead members of his nightwatch team behind, could only mean one of two things: Medina had been kidnapped by the killers, for some reason still unknown, or else he *was* one of the killers.

That would mean he'd been a traitor all along. What in the West was called *uma tupeira*—a mole. If that turned out to be the case…

Camara's men were searching for Medina, scouring the city for a trace of him. So far they had found nothing, but such things took time.

Edouard Camara hoped he had the time to spare.

Quelêle, Bissau

THE LAST PATRONS WERE straggling out of *Flor de Paixão,* which Medina translated for Bolan as the Passion Flower. The club was closing for the night, its diehard drinkers stagger-stepping as they left, supporting one another, talking in the too-loud voices frequently invoked by alcohol as if intoxication threatened deafness. Bolan watched the stragglers lurch off into darkness, while a stocky doorman locked them out and killed the nightclub's neon.

"Passion Flower, eh?"

Medina shrugged. "They come to drink and maybe find a partner for the night. There would have been objections if Camara's men called it the Brothel."

Bolan scanned the street, confirming that the other shops and bars along the block were also closed, no customers or nightly cleaning crews in evidence. He hated collateral damage and took every possible step to avoid it when circumstances permitted.

"Okay, then," he said, and prepared the Semtex. First, Bolan inserted the detonator, one of a half dozen still remaining from the stash they'd found at Storm Transport. One of its wires led to a battery they had acquired in transit from an all-night market that also sold cheap kitchen timers. Bolan completed the circuit, packed his IED into a shopping bag and stepped out of the car.

Medina followed him across the street toward *Flor de Paixão,* covering their advance with his Spectre M4. On arrival at the club's recessed front door, Bolan knelt and set the kitchen timer for two minutes, then retreated to the Peugeot with Medina on his heels. Bolan could hear the numbers running in his head before the plastic charge exploded, taking out the nightclub's door and a substantial portion of the surrounding brickwork.

Bolan took his rifle from the Peugeot's driver's seat and started back across the street, Medina keeping pace with him. A satchel with more Semtex, batteries and timers hung from Bolan's left shoulder, nudging his hip with every stride. He had the detonators in a shirt pocket, well separated from the blasting compound that was otherwise inert.

They reached the sidewalk as the nightclub's doorman came back into view, gape-mouthed and staring at the rubble of the entryway. This time he had a pistol in his hand, and Bolan didn't wait for him to raise it. One shot from the FAL 50.63 knocked his target back and out of frame, into the smoky darkness of the bar.

Bolan cleared the threshold seconds later, with Medina covering his back. They passed the doorman's nearly faceless corpse and moved into the nightclub proper, where the members of a cleaning crew stood cringing over brooms and vacuum sweepers. Farther back, another gunman roared out of a back room, pumping the slide on a short-barrel shotgun. Bolan and Medina fired together, dropping him before he had a chance to aim and fire.

"Let's get the others out of here," Bolan said.

Turning to the task, Medina shouted at the janitors, *"Saia enquanto você ainda pode!"*

They were quick to take the hint, taking their gear along as they departed from the nightclub in a rush. While they were clearing out, Bolan surveyed the place, deciding where to place his charges for maximum effect. Behind the bar, for one, where alcohol would fuel the hungry flames, and against two pillars that upheld the ceiling's weight.

Already moving as the last of the custodians escaped, he went to work.

GENERAL DIALLO TOOK the call reluctantly, listened, then grunted at the caller and hung up. There was no option but to listen when a colonel of the Special Intervention Force called to report another raid against Diallo's interests in Bissau. Edouard Camara would be calling shortly, he supposed, with a redundant message, and Diallo meant to find out why the gangster hadn't solved their problem yet.

In combat, swift solutions were the answer to most difficulties. Find an enemy and annihilate him without mercy. General Diallo saw no reason why the present circumstances should be any different, simply because his adversaries didn't wave a flag or dress in uniforms.

Camara disappointed him. If that continued, he would have

to think about installing a replacement after he had planted Edouard in a shallow grave.

Three strikes within a period of hours meant that someone was determined to upset Diallo's operation. As to why—a profit motive, politics, some personal vendetta—he was at a loss to say. When the attackers were identified, hopefully caught alive for questioning, Diallo would have answers and would seek out those responsible for his discomfiture. Meanwhile, he needed to increase security around his residence and headquarters, in case the enemy was crazed enough to strike at him directly.

It wasn't a likely prospect, but his predecessor was deceased because he failed to take account of desperation and the lengths to which madness may drive a person. Privately, Diallo blessed the bombers who had taken out the man and thereby cleared his own path to command, but he wouldn't repeat the former army chief of staff's mistake. Diallo was an expert at protecting Number One—the *only* one who truly mattered in his world.

His phone rang right on schedule, Camara on the line, prepared to brief him on the nightclub raid and bombing. Coming hard behind the drug-plant raid and the destruction of Camara's secret arsenal, it had the mobster shaken. Diallo heard it in Camara's voice, a sign of weakness that his caller couldn't manage to suppress entirely.

Weakness that could jeopardize Diallo, in his turn, unless it could be overcome.

"What steps are underway to find the men responsible?" Diallo asked.

"Searches of hotels, General," Camara said, "along with questioning of street informants."

"You believe this white man is a member of some local gang?" Diallo challenged.

"No, sir, but if a European team is active in Bissau, they will have been observed."

"Certainly," Diallo said. "My own inquiries at the airport are continuing. About two dozen whites were checked through customs in the past two days. They will be traced to their respective lodgings, placed under surveillance and collected if it seems appropriate."

"Between us," Camara said, "I believe we can prevent further attacks."

"If we cannot," the general replied, "changes will be required. Good hunting, Edouard."

Diallo broke the link before Camara could say more, leaving him with the not-so-subtle threat. Fear was a first-class motivator, and he wanted every man below him in the ranks intensely motivated now, until the challenge to his personal authority had been resolved.

Until the challengers were dead and gone.

CAPTAIN JOSEPH MANSARÉ had given up on going home this night, deciding he would rather sleep on the old sofa in his office than to drive home for a few hours of restless tossing and turning in bed. Reports of violence were coming in more regularly now, but there was still no word about his missing agent. He was prepared to write Nilson Medina off as dead, but the disappearance nagged at him. Why was Medina not among the others who'd been found inside the cocaine cutting plant?

Mansaré actually managed to doze off, and had embarked upon a nightmare that involved hyenas in the streets, when he was jarred awake by the insistent shrilling of his office telephone. He nearly tumbled off the sofa, then caught himself and scrambled on all fours to reach the desk, cursing along the way.

He was panting by the time he lifted the receiver, on its fourth ring. *"Sim? Olá?"*

"Captain Mansaré?" his caller asked.

In a small department like the Judicial Police, ranking leaders typically knew all of their officers by name. Mansaré couldn't claim to recognize their voices on the phone, but this time he was driven by a hunch—a hope—to say, "Medina?"

"Yes, Captain."

"So, you're alive," Mansaré said, stating the obvious.

"I am."

"We've tried to reach you on your cell phone, and at home."

"I've been out of touch," Medina said, sounding evasive.

"You're aware of what's been going on tonight, I take it?" Mansaré asked.

"Yes, sir. I have been…involved," Medina answered.

"Oh? Will you explain that, please?"

And so Medina did. He told Mansaré of arriving at the drug plant with some kind of raid in progress and discovering the man responsible was an American and not a rival gangster. In that moment, suddenly confronted with a choice of who to kill, Medina had abandoned his assignment, shot the other members of the team and helped the stranger to escape. Now they were colleagues, it appeared, waging some hopeless two-man war against Edouard Camara's syndicate and, at least by implication, against General Diallo and the nation's army.

"Have you lost your mind?" Mansaré asked Medina.

"It may seem so," his caller replied. "But I feel completely sane."

"That's often true of lunatics," Mansaré said. "You understand that you're committing suicide?"

"I realize that my career—"

"We're not discussing your *career*," Mansaré interrupted him. "I mean that you've condemned yourself to death for this…this…*estrangeiro*."

"He's foreign to you," Medina replied, "not to me, now."

Mansaré's mind was threatening to overflow with questions. "So, who is he? Who does he represent? Which agency of government? Is this an act of war against Guinea-Bissau? Why does he—"

"Captain, just a minute, please."

When Mansaré was quiet, Medina replied, "I have his name, but cannot share it with you. As to agencies, it may seem strange, but we haven't discussed it. It seemed to make no difference at first, now even less. As to the war you ask about, I don't believe he plans any disruption of the government, beyond removal of Edouard Camara and the men behind him."

"Only that?" Mansaré asked. "It should be simple, then."

"It sounds ridiculous, I know," Medina said. "I doubt that

we'll survive it. But I feel that I've accomplished nothing up to now." Medina spoke to someone else, English, in an aside, muffled, then came back on the line to say, "I must go now."

And he was gone. Captain Mansaré listened to the dial tone for a moment, then hung up.

"God help you, then," he told the silent room.

"HOW'D HE TAKE IT?" Bolan asked Medina.

"As you might expect," the cop replied. "He says that I'm committing suicide."

"You know," Bolan said, "there's no reason why you can't drop out right now. Assuming that the job's a wash, you could relocate. I could likely help you out with that."

Medina seemed to think about it for a moment, then looked down and shook his head. "This is my home. I will not run away."

"Maybe a new assignment, then," Bolan suggested, "if your captain goes along with it."

He'd been against the call to start with, but had kept his reservations to himself, suggesting that they use one of the city's public telephones to keep police from targeting Medina's cell phone. Beyond that, it still had to be Medina's call on how and when he dealt with his superiors.

"There is no going back," Medina said. "I know that now. No going back and no escaping."

"Makes a pretty dismal picture," Bolan said.

"But we still have a chance. You wouldn't be here if you didn't think so."

"What I think's irrelevant. Win or lose, I won't be staying here."

"But you believe we *can* win." Medina stated.

"What I'm asking you to think about is afterward," Bolan replied. "Let's say we're both still standing. What comes next?"

Medina frowned, shrugged, answered, "I have no idea."

"Something you should consider," Bolan said. "There'll always be someone standing in line to take Camara's place. Same with the general. On top of that, you've got the other drug lords and whoever they've paid off inside your own department, plus the Special Intervention Force. What makes you think you *can* live here?"

"I'm taking it one step at a time," Medina said. "Like you."

"I also look down range," Bolan informed him. "I have exit strategies in place before I start. No job's supposed to be the Alamo."

"But how—"

"My point is that I always plan to walk out on the other side alive. Someday I won't. Okay, I get that, but you're just another kamikaze if you go in feeling hopeless."

"I have hope," Medina said. "I hope to rid my country of Camara, the *escória* that serves him and perhaps a general. I've found out that I could not do it with the law, but you've shown me another way."

"Well, you're ambitious, anyhow."

"My captain, the Judicial Police, will offer no assistance," Medina told him.

"No. I never thought they would," Bolan replied.

"I had a faint hope. Call it fantasy."

"Okay, I won't say this again. You want to drop all this, we can split up right now. Whatever happens, no one on the other side will get your name from me."

"We're wasting time," Medina said. "What is the next stop on the list?"

7

Bairro Militar, Bissau

Major Sérgio Ocante popped his second eight-ounce can of Forever Active Boost, a combination of guarana—twice the caffeine found in coffee—and other assorted ingredients brewed up by Russian chemists with their eyes fixed on Olympic gold. He was exhausted, but the drink invigorated him and left Ocante feeling that he could persist in working for a few more hours, on into the light of a new day.

For all the good that it was doing him.

He still had no leads on the men responsible for wreaking havoc in Bissau since sundown, and he knew that General Diallo viewed no news—at least, in this case—as bad news. Diallo might not literally shoot the messenger, but every time Ocante had to tell his boss that no new information was forthcoming, he could feel his own star dimming. How much longer, then, until it flickered out entirely and he was replaced?

The silver star of a commandant, equivalent to the West's lieutenant colonel, had been within Ocante's grasp until the latest mayhem had erupted in the capital. Ocante had no personal responsibility for any of it, but he had been ordered to collect intelligence and lay out countermeasures, just in case Edouard Camara couldn't do the job himself.

And so far, he had failed.

The notion of a white man running loose in Bissau, picking off Camara's men like targets in a shooting gallery, be-

mused him. Airport records had been scanned, Caucasian
tourists trailed to their hotels and most of them accounted for,
though two or three remained elusive. The others would be
found soon, but Ocante worried that they wouldn't solve his
problems. There were other ways to enter Guinea-Bissau—
any country—and a covert operative from a hostile land would
surely be aware of them.

So far, Ocante only knew the man he hunted couldn't be
what Western journalists would call a "loner." It would take a
lunatic to challenge the Camara Family without support, and
if the shooter was insane, he'd be in custody or dead by now.

Say *dead,* and stop at that. If he was held for questioning,
who knew what he might say?

Ocante ran the mental list of likely sponsors for an all-out
war against Camara. He eliminated agents of the navy and air
force, since their commanding officers had forged a truce of
sorts with General Diallo. After ticking off the likely syndicates from Europe and America, he thought about the other
side of things, the law enforcement agencies that might have
grown fed up with Guinea-Bissau's reputation as a narco state.

There was the CIA, of course, and Britain's MI6, both capable of mounting operations of this sort on foreign soil. Rus-
sia's Federal Security Service was another possibility, though
it required a coin toss to decide if they'd be acting to prevent
drug imports or secure a monopoly for their native *Mafiya.*
The French Directorate for Defense Protection and Security
was a dark-horse candidate for intervention, along with Ger-
many's Federal Intelligence Service. Ocante considered, then
dismissed, Italy's External Information and Security Agency
and Spain's National Intelligence Center as mutually inept.

And other candidates? Ocante couldn't say how many agencies were active in America under the wide umbrella of Homeland Security, or under Britain's Home and Foreign offices.
Covert intelligence, by definition, meant that other nations
were supposed to be kept ignorant.

The major was en route to get an early breakfast, then return to work. He reached his car, had key in hand, when a

shadow-shape appeared beside him and a pistol nudged his ribs. Before Ocante had a chance to speak, the stranger said, "Good morning, Major. If you wish to live, raise no alarm. We're going for a ride."

THEY COULDN'T USE Medina's safe house for interrogation, but he had another place in the Alto Crim neighborhood, located southwest of downtown Bissau. En route, with their captive wedged into the Peugeot's trunk, Medina explained that *Alto Crim* translated as "High Crime." It seemed an odd name for a district of the capital, and Medina had no explanation on tap. The houses that they passed were small but well maintained, shaded by trees in many cases, some with plots of ground laid out for gardens. Farther south, as they approached the Geba River, homes gave way to cultivated land, then coastal marshes. There, on the river, Medina surprised Bolan by directing him to a houseboat, moored to a rickety dock.

"Your home away from home?" Bolan asked.

"One can never be too careful," Medina replied.

They retrieved Major Ocante from the trunk, leaving his blindfold on until he was aboard the boat. Belowdecks, one room served the vessel as a combination lounge, kitchen and dining area. The head and sleeping quarters were located forward, masked by accordion doors. Medina led their captive to a simple chair, removed his handcuffs long enough to seat the man, then pinned his hands behind the chair's straight back before he took the blindfold off.

"Você cometeu um erro grave," the prisoner said.

"English," Medina ordered, standing two paces in front of him.

"I said you've made a serious mistake," the handcuffed man repeated. "I am—"

"Major Sérgio Ocante," Bolan interrupted. "Aide to General Diallo. Have I got that right?"

Surprised, the soldier nodded. "If you know that," he pressed on, "then you must know the danger that you face. Release me now, and I will intercede on your behalf."

"No, thanks," Bolan replied. "We need some information, and you seem like someone who can help us. If you can't, I guess we'll have to try somebody else."

"After you're dead," Medina added.

"Information? On the general? What makes you think that I'd cooperate?"

"Survival instinct," Bolan said. "I'm hoping that you're not a masochist and haven't got a martyr complex."

"*Masoquista?* No," Ocante said. "But I do have a soldier's pride and honor."

"How does that work out with running drugs?" asked Bolan.

"What do you know of life in Guinea-Bissau? Ask this one," Ocante said, nodding in the direction of Medina, "what it takes to live."

"That wouldn't be the pride and honor that you mentioned," Bolan said. "Sounds more like cashing in on misery to me."

"Americans. Always so righteous, eh? Telling the other nations how to handle their affairs. You don't care how our people live, as long as we provide cheap labor and resources for your corporations."

"Cocaine," Bolan said, bringing the soldier back on topic. "You import it from Colombia, with heroin from Mexico, and ship it out to Europe, to the States, wherever. What we need, right now, is information on the next delivery."

"I tell you nothing," said the prisoner. *"Vá se foder."*

Medina turned to Bolan, frowning. "He is tough, this one. Maybe I need my tools."

Headquarters of the Forces Armées de Guinée-Bissau, Bairro Militar

"MISSING?" GENERAL DIALLO blinked at the messenger standing before him. "What do you mean, *missing?*"

"Sir," the young lieutenant answered, "I have checked the building, everywhere. Major Ocante left ninety minutes ago to get breakfast. We expected him back within the hour. The staff at the officer's club never saw him, and his car is in the parking lot outside. He's simply…gone."

Diallo nearly asked what the lieutenant meant by *gone,* then realized that he would be repeating himself. It never paid for the man in charge to look foolish. Instead, he said, "And you've looked *everywhere?*"

"Yes, sir. The offices, of course, both his and every other on the floor and those adjacent. Plus the toilets and the break room with the cots."

"He'd damn well better not be sleeping," the general said, masking his worry now with anger. "Has his car been moved since he checked out for breakfast?"

"I don't know, sir. It is in his designated parking space, as usual."

"And have you checked the tapes, to see whether he actually left the premises?" Diallo asked.

The young lieutenant blinked at him, swallowed and said, "No, sir. That is my oversight. I'll see to it at once."

"Do that," Diallo said. "And come back here directly afterward."

"Yes, sir!"

While he waited, General Diallo smoked a Romeo y Julieta cigar from Havana, the fat Churchill brand that retailed for seventeen dollars apiece. They normally relaxed him, but this night—make that this morning—he remained on edge, unable to decipher where his personal assistant could have gone at such an hour. True, Ocante was a well-known ladies' man, but he wouldn't invite Diallo's wrath by pausing in the middle of a crisis for sex. He was levelheaded, generally serious and devoted to the advancement of his own career.

Twenty minutes later, when he'd finished nearly half of the cigar, a tapping on his office door drew General Diallo from his gloomy thoughts. "Enter!" he said.

The young lieutenant's face looked drawn and harried now, and was there just the bare suggestion of a tremor in his hand as he saluted?

"Well?"

"Sir, on the tape…a man…that is, it seems Major Ocante was abducted."

"What?"

"His vehicle is parked within range of a camera that scans a portion of the parking lot. It sweeps across some forty-five degrees, so that it is not focused on his car exclusively, but—"

"Just get on with it!" Diallo ordered.

"Sir, the tape reveals a man approaching him, then leading him away. We cannot see the second party's face, or where they went beyond the camera's line of sight."

"You said *abducted*."

"Yes, sir. There appears to be an object in the second person's hand that may have been a pistol."

"May have?"

The lieutenant shrugged, half cringing. "Sir, the quality of video is not the best. There may be some way to enhance it, but—"

"And show this other person's face?"

"No, sir. Not from the angle he was photographed."

"Damn it!" Diallo spit the curse. "Then can you say what sort of man he was, at least?"

"What sort, sir?"

"Black? White? *Anything?*"

"Sir, he was African. We know that much. A little taller than the major. Slender, in civilian clothes."

"And no one noticed him skulking about before the kidnapping?"

"No, sir. Apparently, he just came up as if from nowhere."

"Listen well, Lieutenant. I don't give a damn where he came from. What I want to know is where he took Major Ocante. Find that out, or don't come back!"

MEDINA'S TOOLS INCLUDED PLIERS, wire cutters, a claw hammer, a plane, two chisels and a propane torch. He laid them out in line before Major Ocante, on a table where he'd eaten many meals in solitude.

"You do this often?" Bolan inquired.

"I handle most repairs myself," Medina said. "It's not so very different. Dismantling instead of mending."

Looking up from the array of implements, he asked Ocante, "Do you feel like speaking now?"

"Fuck you," the major said.

"As you wish. I'm not a surgeon, Major, but my training has included courses on anatomy. To kill efficiently, as you must know, a knowledge of the body's working parts is mandatory."

"I will say nothing, whoreson."

"In your position, I might spare the insults," Medina said. "But I understand we all have different temperaments. My goal this morning will not be to kill you, Major, but to cause sufficient pain that you may reconsider your decision not to speak. The torch—for now, at least—will minimize the loss of blood. I don't intend to lose you prematurely."

"Listen," the major said, sweating now under the lights. "If you release me now—"

"Not possible," Medina said. "Whatever promises you make will all be lies. Besides, we still need information on the next delivery of drugs from South America."

"I don't—"

Medina cut him off again, saying, "Edouard Camara lost a large amount of merchandise tonight. The cartel won't excuse it. He needs more cocaine, as soon as possible, to make up for the shortfall. If he hasn't made arrangements with your general already, I'll be very much surprised."

"I don't have access to that kind of information," their prisoner stated.

"Oh, no?" Medina smiled. "You want me to believe the general makes calls for scheduling himself? While you do… what? Bring coffee and a pastry? Listen! It is time you took your situation seriously, Major."

The captive slumped. "I cannot help you," he replied.

"In that case," Medina said, "I'll be starting with your feet." He used duct tape to pin Ocante's ankles to the front legs of his chair, then easily removed the major's shoes and socks.

"You don't march much, I would suppose. A few toes won't be missed."

"No, please!"

Medina reached up for the wire cutters, saying, "Do not humiliate yourself, Major. You know the way to stop this, anytime you care to."

"But the general will have me killed!"

"Your more immediate concern is what *we* mean to do, if you will not cooperate," Medina said.

"I can't betray my oath!"

"Too late. You did that when you started smuggling drugs… how many years ago?"

"I serve my country!"

"No. You serve yourself." Medina eyed Ocante's naked feet and said, "Where shall we start? Which little piggy goes to market, eh?"

"You have made contact? That's confirmed?" Edouard Camara asked.

"The ship is on its way," his caller said. "I've spoken to the captain. Five, perhaps six hours yet, before they dock."

"And all the cargo is aboard?" Camara pressed him.

"He confirms five hundred kilograms, sir."

"All right. Call me the minute he docks, and make sure that you supervise the unloading yourself, with all your men on hand."

"You need have no concerns about security, sir."

"You're right," Camara said. "It's *your* concern. And your head if you fail."

He hung up then, before the caller could respond, preferring that the threat be his last word. Camara turned to Aristide Ialá, standing off to one side of his desk, and nodded confirmation.

"How much longer?" Ialá asked.

"Five or six more hours to the island, then unloading, packing it aboard the plane. Another hour for the flight to Penha-Bor. Say early afternoon for the delivery."

"I have a new facility for cutting," Ialá said. "Tight security. We've never used the place before. It's clear."

"You stake your life on that?" Camara asked him.

"Absolutely," Ialá answered, after no more than a heartbeat's hesitation.

"Let that be the price of failure, then," Camara said.

He was in no mood to be generous or optimistic, after three strikes overnight had cost him dearly. Now, he had to recoup his losses by cutting the new cocaine shipment more than usual, stretching it further to cover his costs for the shipment he'd lost. No break on price from the Colombians, of course. They didn't care if he lost product on his end or snorted all of it himself, as long as they received the current wholesale rate of seven million West African CFA francs per kilo. Call it seven and a half million U.S. dollars for the latest shipment, and to profit from it, Camara had to stretch five hundred kilos into two thousand.

Aristide Ialá had already done the math, and now he said, "Some of our buyers will be disappointed by the quality."

"We'll make adjustments," Camara said. "When you supervise the cutting, use a lighter hand for our preferred customers. Take more from the product assigned to street sales."

"You see the risk in that, Edouard."

Ialá wasn't asking him. Street customers, if badly disappointed with the quality of drugs sold by Camara's vendors, might look elsewhere for their shopping next time. If he lost that base, drove buyers to do business with his rivals fronting for the navy or the air force, General Diallo would be angry. Still…

"A risk that we must take, for now," Camara said.

Ialá nodded, whether in agreement or to ward off argument, Camara couldn't say. His second in command clearly wasn't pleased with the current state of their affairs; how could he be? Camara's stomach felt as if he might be working on an ulcer, but it didn't stop him sipping at his coca-leaf liqueur. A man required some comfort in his life, and while the bottle offered precious little, he would take what he could get.

And he would watch his back, meanwhile. The new cocaine shipment should be large enough to keep his operation solvent and assuage Diallo's trepidation for the moment, but Camara knew that he couldn't ensure his own survival without tracking down the man or men responsible for pushing him so near the edge. Each hour that passed with no word from his soldiers on the street was torture, forcing him to wonder what would happen if they never found the enemy. How many more attacks could he survive, before Diallo or one of the city's other drug lords moved decisively against him?

Not much longer.

In a cutthroat business, if you weren't cutting throats, it meant that someone else was primed to slash yours.

His trusted aide, perhaps?

"I would feel better," Camara said, "if you went to supervise the landing of this shipment personally. You can leave at once?"

Ialá blinked at him and said, "Of course. I'll call our pilot now."

One down, Camara thought, if anything goes wrong.

SÉRGIO OCANTE CRACKED before the wire cutters closed on the little toe of his left foot. On the verge of furious, humiliated tears, he blurted out, "Bastard! I'll tell you!"

"So," the man crouched at his feet replied. "You know the question. Answer it."

"There is a shipment coming in today," Ocante said. "Replacing that which you destroyed."

"Delivered where?" the tall American inquired.

"The same as always," Ocante said.

"Make believe that we don't know where that is," the white man said.

Could they truly be so ignorant? Ocante took a deep breath, poised for ultimate betrayal and whatever fate it brought him. "Shipments always come in to Bubaque," he replied.

His captors looked at each other, the American raising an eyebrow. Hunched before Ocante's chair, the man holding the clippers said, "It is an island. One of the Bijagós, known for wildlife in its forest. It has ferry service to the mainland, and there is an airstrip."

"So, the drugs come in by water?" the white man asked.

"Normally," Ocante said. "Sometimes by air from *Costa do Marfim,* but rarely."

"Where's that? The *Costa...*"

"Côte d'Ivoire," the white man's African companion said. "You would say Ivory Coast."

"But *this* load's coming in by ship?"

Ocante knew the question was addressed to him and nodded. "On the *Southern Star,* registered in Liberia. How they receive it, I could not explain."

"Doesn't matter," the American informed him. "Do you have an ETA?"

Ocante frowned until the man holding the wire cutters translated for him. *"Hora prevista de chegada."*

"The arrival time," Ocante said, "would only be confirmed once the ship is closer to Bubaque. I should think sometime in early afternoon."

"And how much is it carrying?" the American asked.

"Five hundred kilos were ordered. You've created an emergency."

"How many guards are stationed on this island?"

"Soldiers, fewer than a dozen," Ocante said. "I can't say how many men Camara may have waiting."

"Can't, or won't?" the American asked.

"I'm helping you!" Ocante said. "We don't consult with him on such things as security, unless he asks for help."

"And there's been no request?"

"I think Camara knows it would be best for him to deal with this himself," Ocante answered. "General Diallo is displeased already, with the losses as they are. Camara knows the saying, '*Salve sua ave antes de parar de bater.'*"

"Save your fowl before it stops flapping," the man crouched at Ocante's feet translated for his companion. "It means take care of what you have, essentially."

"Okay," the American said. "I guess we need to go and see a man about a bird."

"I've helped you, yes?" Ocante asked. "You can release me now."

"And have you warn the general?" The man at his feet drew his pistol as he said, "No way."

8

Bubaque, Bijagós Archipelago

Aristide Ialá still wasn't sure whether he should be disgruntled
or relieved by his assignment to protect and transport the five
hundred kilos of cocaine from Bubaque on to Penha-Bor. It
was a great responsibility, and he knew that the job had only
come to him because Camara knew he would require a scape-
goat if disaster struck again, but it could only help Ialá if he
brought the merchandise in safe and sound. Camara would
claim credit for it with the general, of course, that was a given.
But he couldn't blame Ialá for whatever happened once the
drugs were placed into his own two hands.

Or could he?

No. Camara could *attempt* to shift the blame for any future
mishaps, but Ialá would take measures to protect himself. He
might contact the general directly, brief Diallo on his own
success and start accumulating goodwill with the man who
pulled their strings.

But for the moment, he was focused on the *Southern Star,*
a mile offshore and closing toward the dock Ialá shared with
five uniformed soldiers and fourteen of his own men, all armed
with automatic weapons. Others, wearing knives but otherwise
unarmed, stood by to start unloading the ship's pricey cargo
as soon as the boat had been secured to the dock.

Five hundred kilos, or eleven hundred pounds. Packed in
twenty-kilo crates, the cargo had to be unloaded and removed

from its present packaging, then loaded into duffel bags for transfer to the waiting plane. He'd flown in on a Beechcraft Model 99 with his men, and would be taking him back with him, still a few pounds under the plane's maximum takeoff weight after they'd packed the cocaine on board. Cars would be waiting at the Penha-Bor airstrip, and from that point it was a relatively short drive back to Bissau.

Easy, under normal circumstances, but this day wasn't normal. Anything but. Ialá's future, and perhaps that of the whole Camara Family, was riding on the outcome of this last-minute delivery. Failure wasn't an option.

But it still could happen, anyway.

Warily, he addressed his men, leaving the soldiers to their sergeant. "You are on alert," he told them, "from this moment until we have stored the cargo in Bissau. No one may interfere with this delivery for any reason. If they try, immediately use your weapons. Do not wait for orders. Leave no enemy alive."

In lieu of answering, they charged their weapons, jacking live rounds into firing chambers. All of them were seasoned killers, and Ialá had no fear that they would freeze up under fire, if it should come to that. Ideally, though, the transfer and their takeoff should go down without a hitch. He wanted—*needed*—a smooth operation to assuage Camara's agitation and restore a measure of his confidence, while bolstering Ialá's status as Camara's strong right arm.

They had observed no strangers since arriving on the island, which was good. There'd been no rumors of their latest shipment, and it broke the normal schedule, to throw off any spies. It should be fine, but there was still a yawning chasm between *should* and *would*. The utmost caution was required, and Ialá thought that he was up to it.

What did he have to lose, except his life?

BOLAN HAD BOOKED a charter flight from Bissau to Galinhas in the Bijagós Archipelago, landing on an airstrip used by tourists who wanted to see the old governor's mansion and one-time Portuguese prison. From there, it was a quick run in a

rented powerboat to Bubaque, landing on a beach a half mile
from the island's small airport. Medina helped him drag the
boat ashore and hide it prior to hiking overland through forest rife with monkeys, brightly colored birds and snakes that
wriggled out of sight at their approach.

Bubaque's airfield and its main port were located close together, which facilitated sport fishing excursions and delivery
of cargo that, this day, was scheduled to include five hundred
kilos of cocaine.

Using the various Bijagós islands for deliveries made perfect
sense: foreign transporters weren't forced to show their faces
on the mainland, and whichever military branch controlled
a given island could impose ironclad security. That troubled
Bolan to a point, but he intended to remove this shipment from
Edouard Camara's hands at any cost.

Which didn't necessarily require the drugs to be destroyed.

Bolan had pitched the notion to Medina on their flight from
Bissau to Galinhas. If they saw a way to grab the shipment,
hold it hostage, they might have a chance to draw Camara
out—and maybe put the general behind him in their crosshairs
while they were about it. If a pickup didn't work, their fallback
option was to torch the shipment, send Camara back to square
one with the heat cranked extra high. Bolan thought he could
run with either plan and make it work.

Unless Bubaque turned into a death trap.

Their informant had denied arranging any special military
presence for the coke delivery, and Bolan thought that he'd been
truthful. On the other hand, Diallo could have made the move
behind his major's back, particularly after they had snatched
Ocante from the army HQ's parking lot. The smart move was
to be prepared for anything, and that was why he'd brought the
disassembled RPG along for backup.

Just in case.

The half-mile hike took longer than it should have, moving
through dense undergrowth and watching out for green bush
vipers all the way. Their hemotoxic venom prompted hemor-
rhaging, and no specific antivenin yet existed to relieve the po-

tentially lethal symptoms. Best-case scenario: avoid the snakes
to start with, which meant checking every dangling vine they
saw along their way.

Forty-seven minutes from the beach, Bolan picked out the
sound of voices coming from a point ahead of him. He slowed,
Medina doing likewise, and they crept toward the tree line
where it overlooked a cove and pier where workmen under
guard by half a dozen soldiers and a larger force of shooters in
civilian clothes stood waiting for an aging cargo ship to dock.
Bolan could read the vessel's name in faded paint across its
rusty bow.

It was the *Southern Star.*

Off to their right, some fifty yards away, a twin-engined
plane sat waiting on the single runway of Bubaque's small airport. A man whom Bolan took to be the pilot lounged beside it,
smoking, heedless of the group collected on the pier.

"Plan A?" Medina whispered.

Bolan nodded. "Let them do the grunt work," he replied.
"We'll move in when the plane's loaded, before they get
aboard."

"And then?" Medina sounded anxious.

"Then," Bolan replied, "we see what happens next."

MAURICIO HERRERA TOOK his M4 carbine with him when he
left the wheelhouse of the *Southern Star* to meet the Africans
below. He left behind four of his soldiers armed with Belgian
FN Minimi light machine guns to cover his back, not because
Herrera doubted these particular customers especially, but because he fully trusted no one who was still alive and breathing.

Why take chances, after all?

The leader of the Africans met Herrera at the bottom of
the gangplank, introduced himself as Aristide Ialá and shook
hands. A second member of the greeting party held a briefcase
at chest level, opened it and showed Herrera banded stacks of
ten-thousand-franc banknotes. Herrera riffled through a couple
of the stacks, confirming that they weren't padded with strips
of newspaper, but didn't try to calculate the total in his head.

That would be left to an accountant later on, and if the payment came up short there would be hell to pay.

"It's in the forward hold," Herrera told Ialá. "Twenty-five crates, as was agreed."

Ialá half turned toward his waiting stevedores and rattled off something that sounded like, *"O porão em primeiro lugar, para a frente. Começar a trabalhar."* Herrera knew that *trabalhar* had to be the same as *trabajo*—or "work"—in Spanish, but the rest was gibberish. He thought about the curiosity of two adjoining nations, Spain and Portugal, with common roots but such divergent languages, then shrugged it off as less than insignificant.

Herrera's men would cover the unloading crew, a matter of routine, but there was nothing else aboard the *Southern Star* that they might wish to steal, unless they felt a sudden craving for secondhand tractors earmarked for delivery to Gambia. Herrera had no realistic fear that any of Ialá's men would try to take the money back once they had hauled their drugs ashore. That kind of double cross would lead to killing, and whichever side prevailed this afternoon, it would touch off a war of retribution, drying up the flow of cocaine to the military officers who pulled Edouard Camara's strings. It was unlikely, but his shooters would stand ready with their weapons on full auto, as a hedge against some act of madness no one could predict.

Herrera held the briefcase, nearly smiling at its weight, but stopped short of expressing pleasure in a stranger's presence. Killing time as the first crate came down the gangplank, he asked, "Have the people who attacked your cutting plant been dealt with?"

Scowling, Aristide Ialá answered, "That is no concern of yours."

Watching the African through narrowed eyes, Herrera said, "I am concerned with anything that jeopardizes business. Someone who attacks our customers today may come for us tomorrow."

"They are being dealt with," Ialá said.

"I hope so," Herrera replied. "If you need any help…"

"There is no need," Ialá said. "With the army, we have ample forces to contain the problem."

Herrera nodded. "That's good. Because my orders are to bring no further shipments here until the trouble is resolved."

Ialá blinked at that, delayed a moment, then replied, "This news will disappoint the general."

"If you're on top of it," Herrera said, "there should be no real interruption. By the time another shipment's due, you'll have the bastards wrapped up, eh?"

"I'm confident of it."

"So, it won't be an issue. And if you're still hunting them… well, it is best if you focus on that."

Ialá clearly wanted to respond, even to argue, but he held his tongue. A quarter of the twenty-kilo cases were already stacked up at the far end of the pier, two of Ialá's shooters opening one at a time, removing packets wrapped in oilcloth, stuffing them into the first of several duffel bags that lay beside the crates. Herrera marked the nearby plane, assuming that the drugs would be flown inland from Bubaque.

He raised the briefcase slightly, told Ialá, "I'll just stow this on the ship," and showed the African his back, climbing the gangplank while his soldiers covered the retreat.

Enough small talk with the native villagers. Mauricio Herrera wanted to go home.

IALÁ FELT HIMSELF RELAX a little as the last crate left the *Southern Star*. He cleared the dock and watched a couple of the old ship's crewmen hoist its gangplank. From the bridge, Herrera and his four machine-gunners still watched Ialá's men repacking the cocaine, placing the first fat duffel back aboard the Beechcraft Model 99.

The sons of whores, Ialá thought, had left him with the task of passing the bad news about the interruption in supply on to his superiors. The cartel's leader could have done that with a phone call, but he'd chosen to avoid a quarrel with Camara or the general. If Diallo was enraged and chose to kill the messenger, it cost the cartel nothing.

Even now the *Southern Star* was moving out to sea, starting its homeward run. A few more moments and it would be out of rifle range, not that Ialá seriously planned to fire on the retreating ship. He had the cargo, and would soon be back in Bissau. That would please Camara and Diallo, even if the news he brought from the cartel didn't.

And he already knew what he'd be told after his masters heard the ultimatum from Colombia. Get out and find the man or men responsible for their embarrassment. Try harder than he had already, leave no stone unturned, squeeze every informant in Bissau for the smallest shred of information that could put him on the trail of those he hunted.

All of which Ialá's men were doing now. He frankly didn't know what other avenues of inquiry they might pursue—though he would never say that to Camara, much less to the general. The one survival tactic in a situation of this kind was self-abasement, abject groveling replete with promises to do more, even if, as he suspected, there was no more to be done.

Ialá feared the only way that he would ever find the men he sought was if they struck again and walked into a trap already waiting for them. Then, if they survived with strength enough to speak, Ialá would discover who they worked for, and he could repay the individuals or agencies behind the series of attacks.

But first things first.

The plane was nearly loaded, one more duffel bag remaining. All the crates unloaded from the *Southern Star* stood empty by the dock. Ialá spit in the direction of the fast-receding ship and turned toward the plane. He flinched as gunfire stuttered from the tree line on the far side of the airstrip, while his soldiers ran for cover.

NILSON MEDINA SAW THE PILOT duck behind his plane at the first sound of gunfire, but the man made no attempt to go aboard or start the engine. Worried that he might try to escape on foot, Medina circled toward the runway, jogged behind the squat control tower and came up on the far side of the plane. Too late, the frightened pilot saw him coming, drew a pistol from beneath his baggy shirt, then saw Medina's submachine gun zeroed on his chest and reconsidered.

"Do you want to die?" Medina asked.

The pilot thought about it for a fraction of a second, shook his head and tossed his gun away.

"Good choice," Medina said, holding the Spectre steady in his right hand, while his left found handcuffs in a pocket of his slacks.

"Sit down," he ordered, "and scoot back against the landing gear, both hands behind your back."

A moment later, he had snapped the cuffs on and secured his man. The pilot wasn't going anywhere unless the plane took off with someone else at the controls and dragged him down the runway. Leaving him, Medina flashed a smile and said, "You should be safe, unless a bullet hits the fuel tank."

"Wait!" the pilot cried.

"Consider prayer," Medina said, running back to join the fight.

His partner, Matt Cooper, had taken down two of the plainclothes gunmen by the time Medina reached a decent vantage point, and he was coming under fire from the remainder of Camara's men, together with the six soldiers in uniform. Medina was behind them, sheltered by the northeast corner of the airfield's control tower, when he took them by surprise.

His first shots dropped a burly first sergeant armed with a Kalashnikov, the soldier dead before he knew he had been ambushed. Tracking on, Medina stitched three rounds across the torso of a private as he turned to face the unexpected sounds of gunfire at his back. The dying man triggered a long burst from his FAL rifle, ripping holes across the control tower's plywood facade.

The other four soldiers were running for cover by then, returning fire as best they could on the move, without stopping to aim. Medina ducked a shot that came too close for comfort, missed his running target with the next burst from his Spectre, then recovered his aim and put the next three Parabellum rounds on target, pitching the runner facedown onto the asphalt.

Three remained from the six-man party, and they'd reached their vehicle, an old flatbed truck with slats on two sides and no tailgate. They hid behind it, covered from Medina's view unless he worked his way around behind them or devised some way to rout them from their shelter.

From a cargo pocket on his pants, he took one of the hand grenades he'd liberated from Storm Transport's arsenal. Medina pulled the pin and made his pitch, saw it fall short, landing within the truck's bed, where it detonated seconds later. One soldier immediately bolted, and Medina cut him down before he'd traveled twenty feet, leaving the dead or dying man to twitch his life away, no longer part of anything that mattered.

Still, the other two remained in place, not firing back, but staying out of sight. Medina palmed a second grenade, let it fly, and this time his pitch was on target. It struck the roof of the truck's two-man cab, then bounced out of sight on the far side, where one of the soldiers yelped as he saw it. Both uniformed men tried to run, but the blast caught them first and they died on their feet, torn by shrapnel.

Done.

Medina turned back toward the dock to help Cooper.

BOLAN HEARD THE SECOND hand grenade explode and flicked a glance in the direction of the Beechcraft, glad to see that it was still undamaged. He had eight or nine guns ranged against him, adversaries short on cover as they formed a skirmish line between the dock and the airfield's runway, but they seemed intent on bagging him regardless of the cost. One in particular was shouting at the rest, berating them in Portuguese and driving them ahead of him, to the attack.

Bolan aimed past the men in front, framing their rear guard "leader" in his rifle sights and squeezing off a double-tap that stole the shouter's breath and voice with a pair of NATO manglers ripping through his lungs. The mouthpiece lurched, dropped to his knees, then toppled over on his left side, while the others ran ahead without him. If they missed his driving voice, it didn't show.

Still sheltered by the tree line, Bolan set about the bloody business of demolishing his enemies. He worked from left to right along the skirmish line, firing short bursts of three or four rounds each, toppling the runners as they came to him, holding his aim despite a storm of automatic fire that raked the trees above him. Tattered leaves and shredded bark rained down on top of Bolan, but he lay unflinching, squeezing off at each of them in turn, resolved to finish it.

Along the line, they dropped and died, traces of crimson hanging in the air for seconds afterward, before it settled over them like grisly rain. Bolan supposed his magazine was close to empty as the last two charged him, screaming incoherently. As he fired, another weapon caught them from their left side, stuttering through what he recognized as the suppressor on Medina's SMG. Converging fire nearly prevented those last two gunners from falling, but his magazine ran empty, then, and finally released them to collide with the earth.

Medina crossed the battlefield, scanning for stray survivors, as Bolan emerged from the trees. No one remained to challenge them, and when he looked to sea, the *Southern Star* had vanished from his sight. With no one left to kill, he turned back toward the plane.

"You got the pilot?" Bolan asked Medina.

"Waiting for us," his companion said.

"Okay."

Camara's men had dropped one duffel bag of coke when Bolan started firing at them. He retrieved it from the tarmac, lugging it along to put it in the Beechcraft, while Medina freed the pilot from his cuffs and walked him back to Bolan.

"You speak English?" Bolan asked him.

"Yes."

"So, here's the deal. You fly us and the cargo where you're told, no funny business, and we'll let you go, together with the plane."

The pilot frowned and asked, "What is this 'funny business'?"

"Truques ou problemas," Medina said, translating.

"Ah. No tricks or trouble. I agree, most certainly," the fly-boy stated.

"We're good to go, then," Bolan said.

He turned to Medina. "Will you give him the coordinates?"

Medina nodded, rattling off their destination in his native Portuguese. The same spot where they'd caught the charter flight from Bissau to Galinhas, where his car was waiting. And from there...

Well, they would have to see what happened next.

9

*Headquarters of the Forces Armées de
Guinée-Bissau, Bairro Militar*

"You have something for me?" General Ismael Diallo asked
his caller.

"I do," Pascal Kinte replied, "although I'm not sure if it
helps you."

"I will be the judge of that," Diallo said.

"Of course." Kinte cleared his throat, then said, "The man
you're looking for, I've learned, was working under cover for
the Ministry of Justice. More specifically, the Judicial Police."

Diallo clenched his teeth, squeezing the telephone receiver
in a death grip. "You are certain?"

"There's no doubt," Kinte said.

"How long?"

"I have no date, precisely, but if he attached himself to the
Camara Family, we may assume it was a plan to infiltrate the
operation."

Diallo snarled a curse. "Who does Barbosa think he's tri-
fling with?"

"Don't jump to any rash conclusions, General," Kinte said.
"Nothing I've learned so far suggests the Minister of Justice
authorized this plan, or even knew of its existence."

"He's supposed to be in charge, goddamn it!"

"As are you," Kinte said. "Does that mean you're aware of
everything your sergeants do, around the clock?"

"It's not the same!" Diallo snapped. "If he attacks Camara, he's attacking me!"

"Which leads me to believe that he was kept in ignorance by one or more of his subordinates."

Diallo thought about that for a moment, then said, "Very well. I need to know who authorized the infiltration."

"I know that, as well," Kinte replied, stretching it out. "A captain of the Judicial Police, one Joseph Mansaré."

"He's assigned to headquarters, I take it?" Diallo asked.

"I assume so," Kinte said.

"All right, then. I'll take care of it."

"With circumspection, eh?" the Minister of the Interior suggested. "We already have the world's eyes watching us. The last thing that we need is the appearance of another coup."

"I don't need a coup to deal with one police captain," Diallo said. "Much less his sneaking stooge."

"The bad publicity—"

"Is my concern," Diallo said, cutting him off. "I've noted your opinion. Don't belabor it."

"In that case," Kinte answered stiffly, "if there's nothing else?"

"Nothing," Diallo said. "Goodbye."

Diallo would have slammed the old-style telephone receiver into its cradle, but he had been working on his self-control of late, aware that blinding rage wasn't productive. Later, if he still was in a mood, Diallo reckoned he could slap around one of his wives as a release of pent-up tension. Or perhaps he'd simply take the youngest pair of them to bed, if the distractions of this endless day allowed him to perform.

Meanwhile, he had the names of two men who had plotted to destroy him, and he meant to punish both of them. The captain should be easily locatable. As for his agent who had dropped from sight, perhaps Joseph Mansaré had some means of reaching out to him.

If so, the captain would reveal it. General Diallo had no doubt of that. His men were most persuasive when they put their minds to it, and in the present case they would apply themselves with special zeal. If need be, they could make a stone recite the Lord's Prayer.

Diallo thought he might enjoy watching them work this time.

In fact, he might invite an audience, as an example to subordinates who let a stray thought of disloyalty linger in their minds, to nip it in the bud.

For the first time in what felt like days, Diallo smiled.

THE AIRSTRIP AT MINDARA was located near Estrada da Granja do Pessube, northbound into central Bissau. Bolan and Medina cuffed their hostage pilot to the plane's control yoke while they shuttled its illicit cargo into Bolan's rented car, parked out of sight from the Beechcraft's cockpit. The flyboy could take off from there or radio for help, whichever he preferred, but they were off and rolling into town without allowing him to glimpse the Peugeot or its license plate.

"No second thoughts about this stash?" Bolan asked as they turned off onto Avenida de Centura, rolling northeastward.

"It is my last safe house," Medina said. "I rented it under another name. No one else knows that I'm connected to the property."

"Sounds like you planned ahead for trouble," Bolan said.

"In Guinea-Bissau, one must *always* plan for trouble," his passenger replied. "The military might depose our president tomorrow or the next day, and disband the Ministry of Justice. Who can say? It's best to be prepared."

"Who do the neighbors think you are?" Bolan asked.

"No one," Medina told him. "They don't care, don't think about it. They have problems of their own."

The house was small, squatting behind a square of dead grass masquerading as a lawn. Bolan followed a double set of tire ruts to a frail carport in back, surveyed the homes to either side and saw no evidence of anyone observing them. It took two trips for each of them to clear the Peugeot's trunk of duffel bags stuffed with cocaine.

Inside, Medina led him to a closet door, as it appeared, which opened onto stairs descending steeply. An unfinished basement lay below, its dirt floor boxed by walls built out of cinder blocks. There was a table, maybe once intended as a work bench but ignored while it collected dust. They placed the duffels there, instead of on the floor, and left them in the dark when they were done.

"No burglars in the neighborhood?" Bolan asked as Medina locked the basement door.

"I've had no problems in the past."

"Okay, then."

"You will reach out to Camara? Or Diallo?"

"Let them stew a little, first," Bolan replied. "We have some cages left to rattle, yet."

"They will be searching for us," Medina said.

"I'd expect no less. How badly are you compromised, back at the ministry?"

Medina thought about it. "I don't believe my captain will betray me."

"Don't believe it, or don't want to?" Bolan asked.

Medina shrugged. "Of course, it is a question of the pressure brought against him. He could lose his job and benefits, such as they are, for trying to protect me. Still, I trust him."

"Fine. But is there anybody else?"

"Captain Mansaré kept my mission to himself for just that reason," Medina replied.

"Nobody else knows you were under cover?"

"No."

"Where do they think you are right now?" Bolan inquired.

"I doubt that many think of me at all," Medina said.

"Well, someone will," Bolan replied. "Camara must be wondering what's happened to you at the cutting plant. He'll start to ask whoever he can think of, if he hasn't yet. And if he has connections on the force—"

"He does," Medina granted.

"Well, then. You know the saying that you can't go home again?"

"I understand it."

"So," the Executioner told him, "we may as well go make some noise."

THE MAN STANDING before Edouard Camara's desk was clearly frightened, and with reason. He had lost five hundred kilos of cocaine and had watched fifteen of Camara's best soldiers gunned down, including his second in command, without lifting a finger to stop it. Now he begged for mercy, rheumy eyes welling with tears.

Camara, seated with the desk between them, glared holes through his unexpected visitor. "You're certain Aristide is dead?" he asked.

The pilot bobbed his head. "Sir, there is no doubt. I saw him fall, shot down."

"And all the others," Camara said.

"Yes, sir."

"While you were…what's the story? Handcuffed to the airplane's landing gear?"

"It's true, I swear!"

"You *were* armed, were you not?" Camara asked.

Another nod. "I was, but I am not a gunman. Suddenly, a man was there with a machine gun, telling me to drop my pistol. What else could I do?"

"You could have killed him, or died trying," Camara said. "But instead, you helped them steal my merchandise."

" No, sir! I did not help them! You must see, I had no choice!"

"And once again, I say, you had the choice to die," Camara answered. "What would they have done without you? Drag five hundred kilos of cocaine to the beach and swim away with it?"

"I did not think."

"I see that," Camara said. "These two men. You say that one was African, the other white, perhaps American."

The pilot nodded rapidly, eager to please.

"What else did you observe?"

"Sir?"

"Their vehicle, for instance, when they left the airfield. Did you see it?"

"There was no opportunity."

"Or you were frightened. Maybe kept your eyes closed when you *could* have seen it?"

Furious head-shaking. "No, no, no!"

Camara sighed. "All right, then. I believe we're finished here." Half turning to the pair of soldiers who stood waiting by his office door, he said, "The farm for this one."

They moved to flank the pilot, took his arms and started leading him away. Wild eyes, the pilot babbled at Camara. "Farm, sir? What is the farm?"

"Your final destination," Camara said. "Give Gustave Junior my regards."

"Gustave? I don't—"

Then he was gone, for good. It would be a short drive to the small plantation southeast of Bissau, which Camara had converted into a crocodile farm. The hides were sold for expensive boots and other items, but the farm also provided a disposal system for those inconvenient bodies that Camara had on hand from time to time. Gustave Junior was the prize of his collection, a fourteen-foot Nile crocodile he had named for Burundi's notorious man-eater, the original Gustave. Always hungry, he helped Camara rid himself of six to eight men in an average year.

One minor problem solved, but that still left the latest in a string of major headaches. With a second shipment lost, hauled off to who-knew-where, Camara would be forced to answer for it. And he knew the general wouldn't be amused.

Headquarters of the Forces Armées de Guinée-Bissau, Bairro Militars

CAPTAIN ABDOUL LOUA felt zero apprehension as he presented himself to General Diallo's receptionist and waited for confirmation of his appointment. The summons had been sudden, but not unexpected. With so much happening in Bissau and environs, Loua had known it was only a matter of time before the Special Intervention Force became involved.

And he was looking forward to the action.

The FIE, as it was known—for its Portuguese name, *Força de Intervenção Especial*—wasn't a typical police department. And although attached to the Guinea-Bissauan army and commanded directly by General Diallo, it wasn't a military police force either. It fell somewhere between the two, in a murky gray area where politics and law enforcement mingled, a paramilitary team theoretically created to deal with major crimes and threats to national security, but lately employed more often to defend criminal allies of the army's general staff.

Which troubled Captain Loua not at all.

He was a warrior, first and foremost, giving little thought to which side he supported in a given conflict, as long as he was on the *winning* side. This day, in Loua's homeland, that meant backing General Diallo and the army in whatever course of action they pursued. If it included executing meddlers from the Judicial Police or riding shotgun on drug shipments from Colombia, so be it.

The receptionist escorted Captain Loua from the waiting room to General Diallo's private office. Snapping to attention in the presence of his ultimate commander, Loua held his sharp salute until it was returned, then stood rigid in his place until Diallo said, *"À vontade."* Relaxed into the at-ease stance, hands clasped behind his back, Loua waited to hear his next assignment.

"You are aware of the disturbances Bissau has suffered recently," Diallo said, not making it a question.

"Yes, General."

"I've learned that one of those responsible for the disruption is an officer of the Judicial Police. Does that surprise you, Captain?"

Loua considered it, then said, "It does, General. They normally do nothing."

General Diallo smiled at that, then said, "It seems that some of them, at least, are changing. We must locate this officer. *You* must locate him. Capture him for questioning, if possible. If not…kill him."

"Yes, General. His name?"

"Nilson Medina." As he spoke, Diallo slid a piece of paper toward Loua, across his massive desk. "You'll find his address and some other details here, although I don't expect he'll be at home."

"I'll find him, General."

"The search must be discreet, but still effective," Diallo stated. "Choose the best half dozen men available. Keep me advised. Dismissed!"

Captain Loua stood at attention and saluted once again, then pivoted precisely on his heel and marched out of Diallo's office. It wasn't the most exciting mission he had ever been assigned to, but at least it was a start. When he had found this rogue policeman and interrogated him, obtained the names of his superiors and sponsors, there would be more work ahead.

Wet work. The kind Loua liked best.

If he succeeded, he would once again have proven himself to General Diallo. It might even earn him a promotion, if he did the job quickly enough and the results were satisfactory.

And if he failed? Loua dismissed that prospect from his mind without a second thought.

He would succeed because his life depended on it, and he loved his work.

Ministry of Justice, Estrada da Granja do Passube, Bissau

"There was a rented boat," Captain Joseph Mansaré said. "Its owner must be able to describe the man or men who hired it. If he lies about it, bring him in for further questioning."

"Yes, sir," his aide replied. "I'll send the word at once."

"No," Mansaré said. "Go yourself. I want your own impressions of the man and what he saw."

Before his young lieutenant reached the office door, Mansaré's phone rang, clamoring for his attention. Scowling as he snatched up the receiver, he snapped out, *"Olá!"*

"This is the last time I will trouble you," a familiar voice stated.

Mansaré glanced in the direction of his office door, relieved to find it shut. Even so, he dropped his voice an octave as he replied, "I'm not the one who's troubled. If you ask the army, now, the answer may be different."

"I'm trying to avoid them, for the moment," Nilson Medina said.

"That may soon become more difficult," Mansaré cautioned.

"I expect so. Have they mobilized the FIE yet?"

"We're not privy to such orders at the ministry, but it would hardly come as a surprise."

"There will be inquiries about me," Medina said, "if they have not started yet."

"Camara misses you, I know that much," the captain answered. "And I understand that someone from the ministry of the interior has asked for information about any undercover operations we may have in place."

"Were you approached?" Medina asked.

"Not yet. I would deny it all, regardless. Those people do not frighten me."

"They should, Captain. They will stop at nothing."

"And you, my friend? What will you stop at?"

"I'm still learning," Medina told him. "We intercepted a shipment of cocaine, one to replace that which was lost last night."

"Edouard must be having fits," Mansaré said. "I wish that I could see it."

"You should leave the city," Medina told him. "Take your family and get away."

"With what excuse?"

"Pick anything you like. Before we're finished...well, the general may be desperate."

"These seem to be desperate times," Mansaré said. "But honestly, what are you hoping to achieve?"

"I'm not sure," said Medina. "Something. *Any*thing. Expose the full depth of corruption."

"Ah. It hardly qualifies as secret, would you say?"

"Not to our people. To the world. Perhaps they will be forced to act at last."

"And then what?" Mansaré asked. "We become the new Somalia, with so-called peacekeepers and secret operations by the CIA?"

"We have no plans for afterward," Medina said.

"*You* have no plans. But what about your new friend?"

"He is here to do a job. The same we would have done if law and order stood for anything in Guinea-Bissau."

Mansaré knew any further argument was futile—and, in fact, he found himself agreeing with Medina to a point, although the bloodshed troubled him. Particularly when he thought his own blood might be added to the spillage. But if no one ever took a stand, if those who swore an oath to law were satisfied with simply going through the futile motions, then what difference was there between established government and anarchy?

"You said this is the last I'll hear from you?"

"There likely won't be time or opportunity to speak again," Medina said.

"But if there *is,* if you need anything…feel free to let me know."

"Goodbye, Captain," Medina said. And he was gone.

THEY CHOSE THE AIRSTRIP west of Bissau on a whim, a little taste of in-your-face defiance for the hell of it. Medina reckoned that the pilot they'd released would wind up there, and it appeared his guess was accurate. Same Beechcraft Model 99, according to the number stenciled on its rear fuselage, none the worse for wear after its hijacking. There were no cops or other guards around it on the tarmac, nothing to suggest surveillance was in place. The drugs were gone, the flyboy would have been debriefed by now, and might be lying in a shallow grave if Edouard Camara was distraught enough to shoot the messenger.

Whatever.

There was no good reason to destroy the plane, but when

Medina raised the possibility, Bolan had gone along with it. Why not? Replacing the plane with a modern equivalent model—say the Beechcraft Super King Air—would cost Camara six to eight million dollars, depending on where he went shopping. One more heavy blow to both his war chest and mobility, and all that it would cost the Executioner was one five-pound RPG round.

They sat two hundred yards back from the target, perched on a ridge that let Bolan aim his launcher without firing through the airfield's chain-link fence. The Beechcraft had been parked off to the west of the control tower, facing the wire, like a rude student forced to go sit in the corner of his classroom. Camara had no further use for the plane at this moment, no cargo for it to retrieve or transport, and soon he'd be denied his wings entirely.

Loading the launcher as he stood beside the Peugeot, Bolan asked Medina, "Did your captain take you seriously?"

"Yes and no," Medina said. "He understands the trouble that is coming, but he will not leave Bissau."

Some kind of dedication, Bolan thought, and he would be the last man drawing breath to question that. He hoped Medina's captain and his friend, from all appearances—would come out on the other side of it in one piece. That was, if he proved to be the officer Medina took him for. If not…well, he was on his own.

HE AIMED DOWNRANGE, framing the Beechcraft in the launcher's UP-7V telescopic sight. The RPG's original optics, the PGO-7, was basically a mortar sight attached to a rocket launcher, but the newer model was a great improvement, marking the target with a red dot at 2.7x magnification. At his present range, Bolan expected a hit with no problems.

And so it went. When he squeezed the trigger, the launcher fired a jet of flame and smoke behind him, while its warhead flew to close the gap between muzzle and target, trailing its own plume of smoke. Its booster fell away in flight, sprouting a set of stabilizer fins allowing for rotation that enhanced its accuracy. Built to penetrate 260 mm of armor plating, the single-stage HEAT projectile met minimal resistance from the aircraft's fuselage and detonated on impact, devouring the Beechcraft in a roiling ball of fire. The fuel tanks blew a heartbeat later, to complete the job.

Medina laughed out loud and did a little shuffling dance step where he stood. "Camara will be furious," he said, grinning from ear to ear.

"Let's call and break the news," Bolan replied, "as soon as we're a few miles down the road."

10

"Phone call for you, Edouard," Henrique Togna said. He moved to stand beside Camara's desk, cell phone extended like an offering.

"Who is it?"

"He won't give a name," Togna replied. "Says he has information for you on the trouble at Bubaque."

Frowning at the telephone, Camara grudgingly accepted it. *"Quem é esc?"* he demanded.

Instead of identifying himself, the male caller said, "Try it in English."

Camara's frown deepened. "Who is this?" he repeated. "How did you get this number?"

"Numbers aren't a problem," the caller said. "And my name isn't important. I just thought I'd beat the rush and tell you that your drug plane's permanently grounded as of…oh, say five minutes ago."

Despite the spark of panic in his gut, Camara answered with a level voice, smelling the trap. "You've either lost your mind," he said, "or you have called the wrong number. If you have information on a crime, I would suggest you contact the police."

"Well, let me check," the caller said. "You *are* Edouard Camara, right? The narco-trafficker and murderer? Your number is—" He rattled off the digits swiftly. *"That* Edouard Camara? That *is* you?"

Camara felt the heat and color rising in his cheeks. He made a conscious effort to relax his grip on the cell phone as he replied, "You insult me with groundless charges. Once again, I say—"

"Your Beechcraft Model 99," the caller interrupted. "Tail number J5-QZX? You'll need a new one if you plan on any noncommercial flying in the future."

Camara felt his throat trying to close. He cleared it, then said, "I don't understand what you're saying."

"I guess you're not the sharpest chisel in the toolbox, eh? Okay, try this—I just blew up your plane. Call the Penha-Bor airfield and ask, if you don't believe me."

"Hold on." Camara lowered the cell phone and turned to Togna. "Call Penha-Bor and check on the Beech 99," he instructed.

"Check on—?"

"Just do it!"

Camara turned back to his caller. "If what you say is true, why call and tell me this?" he asked.

"I like the personal touch. Full disclosure. I'm shutting you down. If you want to get out with your skin and whatever swag fits in a suitcase, the time to pack up is right now."

Camara had to laugh at that, despite the rage it stirred inside him, burning through his gut like acid. "You're courageous on the telephone. No name, no face. All talk."

"I wasn't talking at your cutting plant," the caller said, "or at Storm Transport. Didn't say a word out on Bubaque. Well, that is, until I told your pilot where to take me with your cargo."

"Cargo?"

"You want to tap dance?" the stranger asked. "I'm not taping anything you say. I'm not police, and in the crazy system you've got here, it wouldn't matter if I were. Okay? You've lost a lot since yesterday. Stay put, and you'll lose everything—your life included."

"I do not respond to threats from strangers," Camara said.

"Suit yourself. But if you're counting on the army to protect you…don't."

"Ah, so you fight the army now, as well?"

"My way," the caller said. "Your General Diallo won't enjoy it any more than you do."

"And if I—" Camara hesitated, listened to the droning in his ear, and realized the line was dead.

Togna came back seconds later, trepidation written on his face. "The plane," he said.

"What of it?"

"Blown up on the runway. By a *rocket,* so they say."

"That son of a bitch will burn in hell!" Camara raged. "He does that, then calls me to brag about it?"

"Who was it, Edouard?"

"How should I know? Do you think the prick gave me his name?"

Togna almost shrugged, then caught himself in time, one shoulder slightly raised.

"But I am going to find out," Camara said. "Today."

NILSON MEDINA'S APARTMENT house stood two blocks west of Avenida Pansau Na Isna, northeast of downtown Bissau. Medina had agreed with Matthew Cooper that it was folly for him to go home, when people had to be hunting him, but he believed they would have checked his flat by now—perhaps ransacked it—and the odds of anyone remaining on surveillance were no more than fifty-fifty. Not the best, but there were things he needed to retrieve, if they were still available, before he could consider any kind of life outside Guinea-Bissau.

His passport, first and foremost. It was hidden in the ceiling, in a plastic sandwich bag he'd taped inside an air duct for the air-conditioner that rarely functioned. Not the most original of hiding places, granted, but it seemed the best available within his dwelling, and Medina chose it over carrying the passport on his person, where it might be lost or stolen.

Also in the flat, tucked well inside the box spring of his sagging bed, were half a dozen other plastic bags containing rolls of banknotes he had squirreled away over the years. Medina had no faith in banks, and while he had checking account at the Banque Régionale de Solidarité, his savings were secured at home. Unless, of course, they weren't.

Medina drove his own car, sidelined since he'd joined forces with Cooper, now sporting fresh license plates he had borrowed from a sedan outside the Hotel Malaka. A bulletin could have been issued for his car by now—likely had been, in fact—but how many aged Toyota Camry compact sedans were tooling around Bissau, wearing patchwork coats of rust and primer paint? Without the proper license tags, he was the next thing to invisible.

Except to those who knew his face.

Medina kept his Spectre SMG on the passenger's seat, stock folded, covered by a two-day-old newspaper. His Glock 19, in its shoulder holster, was closer to hand than the submachine gun, more convenient to use if he was braced by a single opponent. Medina hoped that neither weapon would be necessary on his visit to the flat where he had spent the past four years in seedy solitude, but he would be prepared for anything.

He drove past the apartment house to start with, checking other cars parked on the street, eyeing pedestrians and recognizing some of them as neighbors, though he didn't know their names, had never spoken to them in his life. Some may have known that he was a policeman. As to whether that would make them more or less inclined to trust him made no difference today.

Nilson Medina wasn't hunting; he was *hunted*. With the passport and the money in his pockets, he might have a chance to get away. Without them…

There are always options, he decided.

But he couldn't think of any at the moment.

ABDOUL LOUA WATCHED the Toyota Camry pass a second time and double-checked the license number. It didn't match the plate assigned to Nilson Medina, but what did that prove? Medina was resourceful, an experienced policeman, and at least in size he matched the driver of the car now finishing its second pass by the fugitive's last known address. Loua couldn't have sworn that the man behind the Toyota's wheel *was* Medina, but if he came by a third time there'd be grounds to find out.

Instead of circling the block again, however, the Toyota pulled in to the curb a half block south of where Loua and Sergeant Walkid Rodrigues sat waiting, in a Citroën AX Loua had chosen from the motor pool for stakeout duty. It was gray, thirteen years old and far from memorable, though its engine had been kept in tune and running well. Hidden behind the front seats were their larger weapons, AKMS rifles with folding stocks, chambered in 7.62 mm.

Loua hoped they wouldn't need the rifles. In addition to their sidearms, he also carried a Taser X26 stun gun, capable of firing two darts from an air cartridge over a thirty-five-foot range, delivering a charge of fifty thousand volts to disrupt a target's neuromotor impulses and render him temporarily helpless. While labeled "nonlethal," Tasers had killed in the past by inducing ventricular fibrillation, but Loua wasn't concerned about giving Medina a heart attack.

If the man died, he died. Shit happens, as the Americans would say.

"Get down," Loua cautioned Rodrigues, but the sergeant was already slumped in his seat, reducing his silhouette by half. As Loua did likewise, the Toyota's driver stepped out of his car, scanned the street in both directions, and apparently saw nothing to alarm him. Carrying a folded newspaper beneath one arm, he crossed the street with easy strides.

"That's him," Rodrigues said.

Loua easily confirmed it. "Yes, it's him. Alert the others to stand ready, but remind them *not* to move without my order."

Rodrigues raised his walkie-talkie, keyed it and spoke rapidly to the remaining members of their stakeout team. Their clipped responses signaled understanding of the order.

"Do we let him get inside?" Rodrigues asked.

"It's easier than springing at him now and chasing him around the neighborhood," Loua replied.

"He's likely armed. Something beneath the windbreaker, or folded in that newspaper."

"We won't let him surprise us," Loua said.

"And if we have to kill him?" The sergeant sounded hopeful.

Loua shrugged. "We do what must be done," he said.

Down the street, Medina reached the sidewalk opposite and paused again, then crossed a square of blighted grass to reach the small apartment house, opened the front door without using a key and passed inside.

"Not locked," Rodrigues said.

"That makes it easier for us," Loua observed. "Two minutes, then we bring the others in."

They sat and waited, Loua counting seconds in his head, ignoring his watch while he kept his eyes fixed on Medina's dwelling. The cop's flat occupied one quarter of the second floor, the southwest corner, meaning that his windows didn't face the street. He wouldn't see the team approaching to pick him up.

"Now," Loua said. "Call them in. Let's move."

GENERAL DIALLO HEARD the strain in Eduoard Camara's voice, the pitch all wrong, as if he'd lapsed into belated puberty. Normally restrained, at least when speaking to superiors, Camara sounded now as if he might be moving toward a nervous breakdown.

Something to consider, when the man served as Diallo's link to the cartels that made him fabulously wealthy, with his secret bank accounts growing fatter each week. If he couldn't rely on Camara to control himself and deal with any problems that arose, Diallo knew that he would have to find a suitable replacement.

Soon.

"You're saying that he simply called and told you that he had destroyed your plane?" Diallo asked. "And that he was the man who stole our cargo on Bubaque."

"Yes!" Camara said. "And I confirmed the aircraft was destroyed."

"That is…unfortunate," Diallo said. "What do you plan to do about it?"

There was momentary silence on the line, before Camara said, "I called to ask for your help, General. Without it, I…I don't…I…"

Thoroughly disgusted with the conversation, General Diallo fought the urge to curse Camara as a worthless coward and dismiss him out of hand. There would be time enough for that, he knew, after he'd chosen who should rise to lead the Family. Meanwhile, he had to placate the sniveling insect and keep him on board to repair the damage they'd suffered.

"You're in luck, then," Diallo said, setting an example with his reasonable tone. "I have already made important strides toward solving your dilemma."

"Oh?" Camara sounded skeptical.

"Indeed. I have discovered that your missing soldier from the first attack was sent to infiltrate your Family by the Judicial Police."

Diallo heard a gasp, and while that bitter news sank in, he said, "Now, as we speak, I have men searching for him, under orders that they may not rest until he is in custody. Soon, we will know who put him up to this insanity and punish them, as well. Order shall be restored."

"But if you cannot find him—"

"That defeatist thinking only makes things double difficult, Edouard. You must be *positive*. Be *confident*. Predicting failure is an invitation to defeat."

Camara didn't sound convinced, but he responded weakly, "As you say, sir."

"Now, concerning your arrangement with Colombian suppliers, how soon are you able to replace the lost product?"

"Replace it? Sir, I've spent—"

"The cost is immaterial, Edouard. To stay in business, we need merchandise. The loss is your responsibility. *Two* losses, now, within as many days. If you cannot replace it…"

"Sir, I will! You have my word!"

Diallo's smile was vulpine. "Good. I knew that we could count on you. And always bear in mind, you *must* be positive!"

With that, Diallo cut the link and let his smile retreat into a glower. He was positive of one thing on his own account. Edouard Camara's days were numbered, and the countdown had begun.

NILSON MEDINA FOUND his passport and the money where he'd left them, with no evidence that anyone had been inside his flat since he had left it for his night shift at the cutting plant—how long ago? It seemed like weeks, when barely one full day had passed.

What did it mean, finding his small apartment undisturbed? Was there a chance that Edouard Camara thought he had been killed during the first raid at the cutting plant? How, then, would he explain Medina's disappearance, when the other dead were left discarded where they fell?

At least he knew that Joseph Mansaré hadn't betrayed him and wouldn't. Whatever risks the captain undertook were his own, but Medina couldn't escape a pang of guilt when he considered that his rogue behavior might have jeopardized Mansaré's rank and pension—or his life.

Medina stuffed his cargo pockets with the rolls of franc notes, tucked this passport into his windbreaker's inside pocket and surveyed the flat one final time before leaving. He considered packing clothes, then shrugged off the thought. Departing with a suitcase might make an impression on his neighbors, if any were watching, and he didn't want tongues wagging if—when—searchers got around to checking the apartment. There was still a chance, however slim, that he might manage to return once more, when he and Cooper were finished with their work in Bissau. And if not, he had enough money on hand to supplement his limited wardrobe.

He only lingered on the other option, failure, for a moment, before pushing it away. Medina knew there was a decent chance that he would never need another suit of clothes, but why belabor it? Right now, he needed nerve and ammunition more than shirts and slacks. The quicker he got back to Cooper, the sooner they could be about their business. Finish it, one way or another.

Medina was crossing his small living room, halfway to the exit, when the door crashed open and a swarm of men rushed in. They moved like soldiers but weren't in uniform, all but the leader holding pistols ready, leveled at Medina. There was something pistol-shaped in his hand, too, but it looked odd somehow, off-kilter, not a normal gun. Instead of trying to identify it in the fraction of a second that remained to him, Medina gauged his own odds of survival.

He had tucked the Spectre M4 underneath his arm once more, still swathed in newspaper, and knew he couldn't bring it into play before the unexpected visitors shot him to bloody bits. As for his pistol, it was likewise out of reach. Trying to run would be a foolish waste of time and energy; the only other exit from his small flat was a bathroom window, and Medina knew he had no hope of reaching it.

With nothing left to lose, he bluffed. "I think you have the wrong flat, brothers."

"We are not your brothers," the leader of the pack said. "And there is no mistake, Medina."

"Were we introduced?" Medina asked. "I don't recall it."

"You will have time to remember many things in custody," the spokesman said.

"So, you're police? In that case, let us go, by all means."

As he spoke, Medina moved his arm enough to let the Spectre drop six inches, caught its pistol grip and was about to spin the weapon forward when the leader fired his strange handgun. Two darts hurtled across the gap between them, sank into Medina's chest like viper's fangs, and then he lost control of every nerve and muscle in his body, twitching as if he'd been stricken with a grand mal seizure, dropping senseless to the floor.

MEDINA WAS LATE, and that couldn't be good. Bolan had run the mental checklist of things that could stall a driver in Bissau—traffic snarls, a fender-bender, the police—and had dismissed them all. Medina had a cell phone with Bolan's number on speed dial, and he could have flashed a warning signal in any routine situation. Failure to keep their appointment, plus failure to call, meant he'd run into trouble without time to reach for his phone.

Bolan gave it another five minutes, then wheeled his Peugeot out of the hotel parking lot they had agreed on as a rendezvous point. He had considered phoning Medina, then dropped the idea, unwilling to risk a trace on his cell if Medina's phone had fallen into hostile hands. The flip side was a calculated risk of missing Medina in transit while en route to his apartment building, but the JP officer could call at any time if he was free and clear. The fact that he had not—and that the cell stayed silent during Bolan's drive north across town to Cupelon de Baixo—told Bolan that Medina didn't have the option of making contact.

He found the street with no problem and slowed in passing, casting a quick glance downrange to survey the block where Medina's digs stood. At a glance, he saw a police cruiser double-parked halfway down, around the point where Bolan thought Medina's address should fall. There were no officers in sight, either afoot or in the car, but what did that prove?

In a city with four hundred thousand residents, and hardly any cops to keep the peace, it struck him as peculiar that a squad car would be there, at just this moment, without some connection to Medina. Anything was possible, of course, but Bolan placed no faith in pure coincidence.

Had the Judicial Police staked out his apartment? Medina's last call to his captain hadn't indicated any kind of manhunt underway, but if there was suspicion of a vigilante officer at large, might the investigation bypass his superior until the brass were confident of where the captain's loyalties resided?

Maybe.

Bolan only knew one thing for sure: the worst thing he could do right now was to make a pass along Medina's street and let another officer glimpse his white face, particularly if the police were working with Edouard Camara or the general behind him to nail Bolan and Medina for their moves against the syndicate.

He had one option—not a great one, but it might be worth a try. Medina trusted his immediate superior, perhaps unwisely,

but they'd spoken twice since Bolan and Medina had decided
to collaborate. Medina had provided the Executioner with the
captain's name and phone number, a hedge against exactly what
seemed to be going down this afternoon. There was a risk in
calling him, but Bolan had to know whether Medina was alive,
in need of help, or if he was already gone.

But first, he wanted space between himself and what appeared to be a trap.

He put the quiet street behind him, driving back toward hell.

11

Ministry of Justice, Estrada da Granja do Passube, Bissau

Captain Joseph Mansaré had learned to dread phone calls. No one ever summoned the police to celebrate good times, invite them to a party or report that all was well. The calls that came were angry, tearful, terrified—and most times, there was little that Mansaré or his officers could do to help. Dispatch an ambulance, perhaps, if there was one available. Question eyewitnesses, if any dared to speak. File a report that would, most likely, fail to generate any results.

Mansaré took the calls, regardless, recognizing it as one part of the duty he'd assumed when he joined the Judicial Police. If nothing else, he could shoulder a bit of the tragedy heaped upon his fellow countrymen each day. He could listen, try to empathize. And he could lie, suggesting that things might be better tomorrow.

"Olá," he told the latest caller. *"Capitão Mansaré aqui."*

"One of your men's in trouble," said the caller, male and speaking English.

"Oh?" Mansaré switched languages and asked, "Which one?"

"Nilson Medina. Have you heard from him within the past hour?"

Mansaré felt the block of ice shift in his gut. "Who is this, please?"

"A colleague of Medina's. We've been working on some things together."

"Ah." Mansaré dropped into his chair. "You're the American."

"I'm *an* American," the caller said. "What's happened to Medina?"

"I am not at liberty to—"

"What?" the caller cut him off. "Discuss the case? Save one of your own people while there may be time?"

Mansaré hesitated, shot a glance in the direction of his open office door, checking for eavesdroppers, then said, "He's missing. Until recently, I understand, he was with you."

"He went to get some things from his apartment," the stranger said. "Wouldn't let me talk him out of it. When he ran overtime, I took a look and found police outside of his apartment building."

"They were mine," Mansaré granted. "We received a call from neighbors, some kind of disturbance. When the address came back as Medina's, we were naturally interested. Unfortunately, by the time my men arrived, no one remained."

"So he was snatched, not executed on the spot?"

"If I must guess, it has the earmarks of abduction. Nothing I could prove, at this stage, if it came to that."

"How do you plan to deal with it?"

Mansaré felt his cheeks burn as he answered, "You must understand, without some kind of evidence—at least a physical description of the kidnappers, if they exist—my hands are tied."

"You know who took him, right?" the caller challenged. "It can only be Camara's people or the army that supports them."

"Even hinting such a thing is dangerous," Mansaré said.

"Hinting around has never been my strong suit."

Frightened of the answer, still Mansaré had to ask. "What are your plans?"

"I'll spare you the specifics. Wouldn't want your people getting in the way by accident. Let's just say I'll be lighting up some lives."

"You risk your life for one you barely know? After one short day's acquaintance?"

"How well do *you* know him?" the stranger asked. "You've been watching him build up to this for…what? How many *years?*"

"The system—"

"Needs an overhaul," the caller said. "That's not my job. But while I'm here, I'm taking down a part of the machine."

With that, the line went dead. Mansaré cradled the receiver, left his hand upon it as he said, "God help you both."

NILSON MEDINA WOKE in darkness, his whole body aching, with a smell of oil and rubber in his nostrils. Rocking motions, first dismissed as nausea from being knocked unconscious, finally combined with the pervasive odors that surrounded him to tell him he was locked inside a car's trunk, rolling over city streets. If they were somewhere in the countryside, Medina thought, it would have been a rougher ride.

He tried to move, testing his arms and legs, his muscles achy from the voltage that had crackled through them sometime earlier, and found his wrists were tightly bound behind his back. It felt like wire chafing his flesh, not rope or proper handcuffs. At least his ankles weren't tied, although the confines of the trunk prevented him from straightening his legs or gaining any major leverage.

How long had he been out? It was impossible to say. Blind in the darkness, unable to check his wristwatch, speculation was a fruitless exercise. He had been taken in midafternoon from his apartment; the events returned to him now as fractured images, then merged into a coherent memory. Logic suggested he was still somewhere in Bissau, though he couldn't judge directions from the frequent turns that kept his upset stomach roiling.

Finally, Medina started counting seconds in his mind, something to do while he tested the bonds pinning his wrists and found that he couldn't escape them. Lying on his left side, he could feel his empty shoulder holster, and the folding knife he carried in a pocket of his slacks was gone, together with the rolls of currency he had retrieved from his apartment.

What else could he tell, in his present position?

The car that carried him wasn't an army vehicle. His captors might be soldiers, but if so, they'd come for him without their uniforms or standard-issue weapons. Then again, it made no difference. Camara's men or General Diallo's, either would be bent on first interrogating him, then snuffing out Medina's life.

He was as good as dead. Unless...

He had to have missed the rendezvous with Cooper by now, which meant that the American would try to find him. And upon discovering Medina had been snatched, however long *that* took, what would he do? What *could* he do?

Medina had counted off nine hundred seconds—fifteen minutes—when the car slowed, made one final turn, then coasted to a stop. A moment later, someone popped the trunk lid, the sudden daylight forcing Medina to squint against its stinging glare. Strong hands lifted Medina from his pit and planted him on trembling legs, then urgently propelled him toward an open door. Some kind of warehouse stood before him, and the fact that no one screened it from his view affirmed what he already knew.

They didn't care if he identified the building, since he'd never have a chance to speak of it with anyone. Medina wasn't meant to leave this place alive.

Inside, crossing a concrete floor, he was escorted at a rapid pace until they reached the middle of a spacious empty chamber, echoing with footsteps. Roughly centered in the room, a straight-backed wooden chair sat waiting to receive Medina. As they reached it, someone snipped the wire that bound his wrists, then he was forced into the chair, pinned with the stun gun pointed at his chest from six or seven feet away.

Two others went to work with duct tape, rapidly securing his chest, arms, legs. When they were done, the leader of Medina's kidnappers lowered his stun gun, smiled and said, "My orders are to wring you dry of information. You can save us all some time—and save yourself some pain—by answering my questions honestly."

"And would you take my word for anything?" Medina asked.

The leader thought about it, smiled and said, "You're right. Let's get to work."

BOLAN STARTED WORKING from the list of targets he'd drawn up with Nilson Medina before their raid on Storm Transport. His first stop was a combination brothel and casino, disguised as a health club. Both gambling and prostitution were banned by law in Guinea-Bissau, but that didn't seem to hamper business at the Golden Age Gymnasium.

Bolan wasn't a member of the "gym," and he had no appointment. Neither fact prevented him from dropping in as afternoon bled into evening, finding the joint in full swing. The doorman who met him and reached for a pistol went down on the spot, blood leaking from a Parabellum keyhole in his forehead. The hostess scampered off, shrieking to beat the band, and Bolan let her serve as his announcement for civilian players to evacuate the premises.

As for the staff, he welcomed any efforts to eject him.

When the exit stampede began, Bolan helped it along with an M-84 stun grenade, lobbed high across the chaos of the main casino floor, exploding with a brilliant flash and thunderclap as Bolan kept his eyes averted, distance and the cotton stuffed inside his ears reducing the concussive impact of the blast. He didn't need to hear the panicked players crying out in Portuguese, had nothing to discuss with them as long as they were bent on leaving, and the guards—well, they were absolutely going down.

It turned out there were six of them, besides the late doorman. Bolan saw two appear upstairs, where they'd been keeping track of johns, maybe indulging in some voyeuristic action, while the other four came out of nooks and crannies on the gaming floor. The fleeing customers, dealers and hookers helped confuse them, while the Executioner was marking targets, lining up his shots by order of priority.

He took the closest of the gunners first, with short bursts from his FAL carbine, the first two down and out before they had a chance to use their weapons. The third guy fired his shotgun, splattering a couple of the gamblers who were slow clearing his field of fire, then Bolan dropped him where he stood, while he was jacking up another round.

Next, Bolan shifted to the upstairs shooters, caught them on the stairs, trying to get an angle on him with their SMGs. Before they managed it, he stitched them both and brought them tumbling down to ground-floor level, arms and legs entangled as they hit the bottom and lay still.

Which still left one.

The last man standing grabbed a naked working girl as she ran past him, used her for a human shield, his pistol jammed against her head. It was a risky ploy against a stranger who had come in shooting, lobbing stun grenades, but maybe it was all that he could think of.

And it didn't work.

While Bolan's target shouted threats at him in Portuguese, he aimed and stroked the carbine's trigger once, sending a single NATO round to close the gap and punch the loudmouth's ticket where he stood. The hooker gasped, then squealed an octave Bolan hadn't heard before and sprinted for the nearest exit.

Done…except for bringing down the house.

And with the final cakes of Semtex he had liberated from Storm Transport, that should be a breeze.

EDOUARD CAMARA GLANCED UP at the sound of rapping on his office door, already open, and saw Aristide Ialá's young replacement standing on the threshold, looking glum. Camara almost groaned, but caught himself and asked, "What is it now?"

The young lieutenant, Almami Silva, entered and moved hesitantly toward Camara's desk. "There's been another incident, sir," he said.

Camara felt his stomach clench but tried to keep the grimace off his face. "Tell me," he ordered.

Silva briefed him on the mayhem at the Golden Age Gymnasium. At least six dead, the place demolished with explo-sives, while their customers, dealers and naked working girls scampered over the Luanda neighborhood, dodging authori-ties. Camara didn't want to think about the money it would cost him to set up another comparable operation.

If he even could.

The hammering he'd taken in the past day and a half had clearly shaken General Diallo's confidence in his ability to lead the Family. Indeed, Camara's own self-confidence was wan-ing. What else could he do to salvage his pathetic situation, if Diallo and the army couldn't even find their common enemies?

"All right," he said to Silva. "You've informed me. If there's nothing else…"

"There is, sir. While speaking to our man with the Judi-cial Police, I learned their missing officer has been located."

"What?" Camara's head snapped up, his eyes pinning Sil-va's.

"Rather, I should say he *was* located, but has now appar-ently been kidnapped."

"What?" Camara felt foolish repeating himself, but the news was astounding. The man who had infiltrated his Family found, then abducted? "Explain," he demanded. "What happened?"

"Details are few, sir," Silva replied. "It seems that this Me-dina visited his flat in Cupelon de Baixo and was taken there. Neighbors reported a disturbance. By the time that officers arrived there was no sign of him."

"Taken, but not killed," Camara said. "Why not? You're certain that he's not in custody?"

"Not with his own force," Silva said. "I'm sure of that."

It clicked then, for Camara. Who else would be looking for Medina? Diallo's men. The Special Intervention Force.

But if they had Medina and the general hadn't seen fit to tell Camara, what did *that* mean? Was there any reason to conceal that information from Camara, when a simple thirty-second phone call could have put his mind at ease?

One reason, possibly. And that one amplified Camara's stomachache tenfold.

Diallo had to be planning to dispose of him, perhaps to blame this pig Medina for the deed.

Well, two could play that game.

The general was powerful, of course. But he wasn't invincible.

THE FORTUNE CLUB was a saloon with a backroom bookmaking setup. The building wasn't much to look at, but Medina had told Bolan that the place booked bets on everything from soccer to auto racing, turning a profit for Edouard Camara's syndicate that averaged 480 million CFA francs per year. Call it a cool million dollars untaxed for the Family network.

About to go up in smoke.

Bolan left his Peugeot in the club's parking lot, dusk coming on as he stepped out of the car and took his automatic rifle with him. Pockets heavy with grenades, he crossed the gravel lot and pushed in through the swing door, then was enveloped by the tavern's murky atmosphere. His eyes adjusted quickly, while the patrons sized him up; they spotted the weapon in his hands, and conversation died as if someone had flipped a switch to kill the sound.

Bolan didn't know the phrase in Portuguese, so he used English. "Everybody out! Right now!"

For emphasis, he raised the FAL carbine one-handed, ripped a 5-round burst across the ceiling and then stepped aside to dodge the rush of fleeing customers. The bartender was slower, reaching underneath the bar for something he kept hidden there, and by the time he came up with a stubby shotgun, Bolan had him in his sights.

One round from twenty feet punched through the barkeep's forehead, slammed him backward, bringing down a shelf of bottles that exploded as they hit the concrete floor. Between the gunshots and associated racket, Bolan figured that the backroom gang had to be on full alert, and that was fine.

He wasn't taking any prisoners.

Clutching a frag grenade in his left hand, its pin discarded, he approached the only other door in sight, his carbine leveled when it suddenly flew open and a short man with a shiny pistol in his hand emerged. Bolan triggered a 3-round burst to clear the doorway, made an underhanded pitch with the grenade, then sidestepped to avoid stray shrapnel when it blew.

The blast cut off a symphony of excited voices in the back room, Bolan closing rapidly to peer through smoke and settling plaster dust. He counted half a dozen men scattered around the room, two obviously dead, the others stunned or wounded. The explosion had upended tables, carpeting the floor with betting slips that gave him an idea.

Bolan made one quick circuit of the room, finishing off the four survivors with one point-blank NATO round apiece, then went back to the bar and found some bottles on a second shelf that had survived the barkeep's fall. Returning to the back room, Bolan poured their contents on the betting slips, drew a trail of alcohol across the threshold as he left the room, then found a book of matches on the bar and struck a light.

In seconds flat, the back room turned into a crematorium, smoke rising to the ceiling and expanding there, worming its way into the bar beyond. Destruction of the betting slips, Bolan surmised, would leave Edouard Camara at a loss to say which bettors had been winners on the day's assorted contests, adding one more stressor to the gangster's crumbling life.

A relatively small thing, maybe, but the Executioner would take what he could get.

NILSON MEDINA CLENCHED his teeth and strained against the duct tape that confined him as the cattle prod sent bolts of lightning through his flesh. With each shock, he imagined that his heart had stopped, wondering whether this would be the last time, if it wouldn't start to beat again.

How long had it gone on, so far? Medina had no more idea of that than where he was, in fact. The jolting charges stunned his brain, made him lose count of passing seconds as he tried to push the pain away and hold it at a distance. All in vain, since he couldn't escape the prod or taunting laughter of his captors.

But the man in charge was getting irritated now. The exercise was clearly losing its amusement value. There was anger in his voice as he bent to ask Medina, "Have you had enough?"

Medina spit a glob of blood from where he'd bitten through his tongue, then forced a smile and said, "I'm fine. But make it easy on yourself, if you get tired."

"So, you're having fun? Let me make you happy, then."

The prod came back, jammed in the crease below Medina's navel, and his spine arched with the contraction of his muscles as the voltage seared through them. Medina heard someone squealing, a high-pitched shrilling sound, and realized it was his own voice, taut with agony. The perspiration on his chest and stomach seemed to crackle. He imagined sparks erupting from his flesh.

The prod withdrew, and when its user bent to stare at him again, Medina saw the other man was sweating, too. Was it that muggy in the warehouse, or was he unnerved by Medina's resistance to this point?

"I can keep this up all night, you know," he said. "We have more batteries."

Medina forced a smile that felt as if his cheeks were splitting open. "Good," he wheezed. "I was afraid you might run out."

"You're quite the hero, eh?" his tormentor inquired. "Do you suppose that your American will appreciate the sacrifice? Does he remember you at all?"

"You'll find out when you meet him," Medina said. "I would love to see it."

"But you won't, will you? I doubt you'll be alive that long— or I could fry your eyes out with the prod, right now."

"If it amuses you," Medina answered back.

"Get on with it," one of the other said. "The eyes."

"In a moment," the leader said.

He turned back to Medina, "I am curious, sincerely. Why this loyalty to one who has abandoned you? You've barely known him for a day, and yet you'd suffer all of this—face death—to keep us from him? Why?"

Medina didn't have to force the laughter, and it pleased him, seeing that it took them by surprise.

"You think I go through this for *him?*" he asked. "You're fools. I do it for myself and for our country, to be rid of pigs like you."

The prod man blinked at him and said, "You don't know me."

"I've known you all my life," Medina said. "You've made my homeland what it is today. Now do your worst to me. Your time is almost up."

"We'll see," the other man said, and raised his cattle prod.

12

Edouard Camara knew the time had come to flee his home and find a safer hiding place. It galled him, living like a fugitive, but what else could he do? In theory, he ran Bissau's most powerful crime family and had the full weight of the nation's army behind him, but theory and reality had diverged radically since yesterday. Camara's empire had been shaken to its very roots, and now he had good reason to believe that General Diallo might be turning on him. At the very least, critical information had been kept from him, and what might happen next?

Camara drew no satisfaction from the news that one of his attackers had apparently been captured. How could that console him, when Diallo hid the fact, or when the rogue policeman's comrade still kept striking at Camara's properties?

The Fortune Club was gone now, with its cash and betting slips. This time tomorrow, hundreds of gamblers armed with that news would be clamoring at him for payment, insisting that they had picked winners in this or that game. Camara could dispute it and refuse to pay, but with his staff dead and their records burned to ashes, what excuse could he propose? Even refunding bets would leave him in the red, since he had no idea of how much any given bettor may have wagered.

No. The time had come for him to run and hide. A quick move, without warning or a large phalanx of bodyguards, should do the trick. Downstairs and out, into his waiting car, with just Almami Silva and three men, including his driver. The rest of his force would be waiting when he reached his place in the country, with walls, wooded grounds and defenses to stand off all comers.

He was ready. Picking up the overnight bag he had filled with bare essentials—toiletries, the currency and precious gems from his wall safe—Camara left his office, calling to the others. "It is time! We're leaving! Everyone, come on!"

They rode down in the elevator, hogged the whole car for themselves with no one else complaining, then stepped out into the dusk of early evening. Camara's car was waiting, engine idling, and a sense of sweet relief washed over him as he approached it. Getting out was wise. Whatever happened next, he would respond from safety. From his fortress.

Sudden moisture sprayed Camara's face, a drop stinging his left eye. Was it raining? No. The soldier on his left had fallen, gasping, and Camara realized that it was his blood in the air. His ears picked out the chugging sound of silenced gunshots as more bloody rain descended on him, bodies tumbling to his left and right.

Camara hesitated for a heartbeat, then spun back toward cover, breaking for the tall revolving door of his apartment house. A bullet clipped his earlobe, made him bleat with pain, just as a voice barked out in English, "Freeze!"

Edouard Camara froze. He was afraid to turn and face his killer, but the gunman came to him. He was a white man, tall, athletic in appearance, with a grim set to his face. Camara closed his eyes and waited for the end.

And then his eyes snapped open as the gunman clutched his arm, turned him, propelled him farther down the sidewalk, telling him, "Don't say your prayers just yet. We're going for a ride."

GENERAL ISMAEL DIALLO glowered at the captain standing rigidly before his desk. The young replacement for Major Ocante looked queasy and nervous, as well he might be at disturbing the great man's repose.

"And this stranger said *what?*"

The lieutenant cleared his throat and answered, "That he

would call back within ten minutes, General. To make sure that you were available."

"He gave no name?"

"No, sir. Although he sent regards from…from…"

"Spit it out, Lieutenant!"

"From Major Ocante, sir. And from Edouard Camara."

Diallo ground his teeth together. "So, a man with no name sends *regards* from a corpse and Camara? What else?"

"Nothing, sir. The rest, he said, would be for your ears only."

Diallo considered dismissing the call as a hoax, then decided against it. "In that case," he said, "I will listen, if he should call back. In the event that it is not some stupid prank, make arrangements to trace any incoming calls."

"Yes, sir!"

"Dismissed."

Diallo's phone rang seven minutes later. He delayed responding until it had rung three times, giving the tracer mechanism time to activate. Prepared to speak in English, then, Diallo lifted the receiver to his ear and said, "Hello?"

"Who am I talking to?" the strange voice asked.

"I am the one you seek," Diallo said.

"I understand your people have a friend of mine in custody," the caller said.

"It's possible," Diallo granted, smiling to himself.

"Just possible?"

"I could not verify it absolutely without making inquiries."

"So, make them. Then we'll talk about a trade."

"What do you have that I might want?" Diallo asked.

"Your partner in crime," said the caller. "He's still in one piece, but I'd need my friend back the same way."

"I'm confused," said the general, playing for time. "This so-called partner—"

"Or puppet, whatever," the voice interrupted. "One Edouard Camara."

Diallo lost his smile, considered hanging up the phone at once, then stayed his hand and asked, "You have him with you?"

"Safe and sound. For now."

The plan came to Diallo suddenly, ideal and irresistible. "I fear," he said, "that you've been misinformed. I am the chief of staff for Guinea-Bissau's army, and I have no partners, as you put it."

"I'm not taping this," the caller said, "if it concerns you."

"Nothing that you say or do concerns me. As for Edouard Camara, he is well known as a common criminal."

"Funny no one has managed to arrest him."

"You may be aware of our peculiar system," Diallo said.

"So you're saying—"

"Kill him if you like," Diallo said, "and do us all a favor."

There was fleeting silence on the line, before the caller said, "I'll pass your sentiment along. Should I just go ahead and torch your cocaine, while I'm at it?"

Diallo felt a dull pain start to throb behind his left eye. "I'm afraid—"

"Five hundred kilos," the caller said. "Lifted from Bubaque earlier this afternoon. I'll light it up, if that's your pleasure. Would it be another favor?"

"We should not be too hasty," Diallo said.

"Right. I'll call you back for details on the swap in…shall we say an hour? And I'll be expecting proof of life."

The line went dead. Diallo cursed the silent telephone, then urgently began to dial an number drawn from memory.

ROLLING NORTHEAST ON Avenida di Cintura, with his cell phone switched off to frustrate any trackers, Bolan pulled the strip of duct tape from Camara's mouth and listened to him splutter, cursing what he'd heard when Bolan put the call on speaker.

"So, Diallo wants you dead. What should I do?" he asked the narco-trafficker.

"Kill *him,* the fat *picada.* Or, you let me go and *I* will kill him for you."

"It's a thought," Bolan allowed, "but based on past performance, I doubt you could do the job."

"At least untie my hands," Camara said. "They're grow-ing numb."

"You're all right for a while yet," Bolan said. "It may not matter, anyway."

The mobster swiveled in his seat to stare at Bolan, wide-eyed. "You intend to kill me as he said? A favor to the gen-eral? I thought—"

"Consider it a favor to the country you've been looting, while your people live from hand to mouth," Bolan replied. "I wouldn't give your general a glass of water if he was on fire."

"But you assist him by eliminating me!" Camara blurted out.

"How's that?"

Camara thought about it for a moment, then suggested, "He knows I would testify against him, for betraying me."

"What good would that do?" Bolan asked. "Your country doesn't even have a prison that could hold him."

"But they're building one," Camara answered. "And the charges might not be confined to Guinea-Bissau."

"Meaning what?"

"Aside from smuggling the drugs, Diallo is responsible for various…atrocities, as you would say it…against rural villages and activists who have opposed him. And crimes committed in our civil war, before he rose to chief of staff. He could be tried before the World Court, yes? I have the evidence!"

"You say that now."

"It's true! I've planned against the day when he would aban-don me. I never trusted him."

"And once they've packed you off to Holland or wherever in protective custody, then what? You change your tune and blow the case?"

"Why would I?" Camara asked. "I would then have noth-ing left."

"Except whatever money you've got stashed in banks around the world to tide you over," Bolan said.

"You would have me starve?"

Bolan shot him a glance that made the mobster turn away,

developing a sudden interest in the flow of traffic that surrounded them.

"There's someone I can call," he said, after another mile. "I don't know whether he'll have any interest in your offer, but I'll pitch it to him."

"And if he rejects it?" Camara asked.

"Then you'll be of no further use to me," Bolan replied.

"I will convince him."

"That's your problem. And another one," Bolan said. "If he takes you up on it, and you decide to pull the plug before the case has run its course—"

"I've promised I will not!"

"And I trust you as far as I can throw this car one-handed," Bolan said. "Word to the wise. Renege, and I'll see to it that you don't live to enjoy those offshore bank accounts."

CAPTAIN MANSARÉ RECKONED he would have to spend another night at headquarters, waiting for the reports of bloodshed to come in. Perhaps one of the bodies found would be Nilson Medina's. There was nothing that Mansaré could do about it, no realistic way that he could hope to find or punish any of the perpetrators, but he felt the call of duty to remain and make the wasted effort, anyway.

His first call of the night, therefore, surprised him.

"Any word about Medina yet?" the now-familiar voice inquired, after Mansaré's curt *"Olá?"*

"Nothing," Mansaré answered. He had entertained a fleeting hope that the American might find his missing officer, but dared not say as much.

"I had a word with General Diallo," said the faceless stranger.

"*What?* Have you completely lost your mind?"

"You're not the first to ask me that," the caller said, a trace of wry amusement in his tone. "Let's say the votes aren't in."

"Why would you call the general?" Mansaré asked.

"To see if his men had Medina."

"And he said?"

"Nothing, at first. He played dumb, but I got him with my second offer of a trade."

"A trade? Did you say *second* offer?" Suddenly, Mansaré felt as if he'd lost his place within their conversation.

"Right," the caller said. "He wasn't interested in my first bid, which is why I'm calling you."

"First bid?"

"I offered him Edouard Camara for Medina. Had him on the speaker phone. Camara was surprised to hear his buddy tell me I should waste him."

"Wait. You have Camara with you?"

"That's affirmative. And since he got the brush-off from Diallo, he's decided it might be a good idea to turn state's evidence."

"You mean, to testify?" Mansaré asked.

"That's it. He's talking drugs and international connections, murders, war crimes, take your pick."

"He'll testify against *Diallo?*"

"Against anyone he's ever worked with, from the way it sounds. If there's a court that you can trust, he'll give you evidence. And if there's not, he's willing to go elsewhere."

Mansaré knew that could only mean the International Criminal Court, established in 2002. Guinea-Bissau wasn't a signatory of the statute that had established the court, but if Mansaré could place his evidence before that tribunal somehow...

"Camara will surrender? To me?"

"You pick the time and place," the caller said, "and I'll deliver. Make it fairly soon, though. I still have to call Diallo back and set up our exchange."

"The second bid, you mean. What did you offer him?" Mansaré asked.

"A planeload of cocaine," the caller said. "After the stash he lost the night before last, he was bound to go for it."

"And you will trade these drugs for Nilson's life?"

"Diallo thinks so," the American replied. "I'll have to wait and see how it shakes out."

"You plan to double-cross him, then?" Mansaré asked.

"It's double-*cross*," the caller said, that note of levity again. "I wouldn't want to telegraph my punches. Let's say that the general should trust me just as far as I trust him."

"You don't expect to get Medina back," Mansaré said, his sense of dread returning.

"Stranger things have happened, but I wouldn't bet your pension on a happy ending."

"No," Mansaré said. "I'm not sure I would recognize one, as it is."

"Well, tell me where to drop Camara. Maybe you can work one out, yourself."

"Why not the old American embassy?" Mansaré suggested. "On Avenida do Agosto. Shall we say one hour?"

"We'll be there," the caller said, and cut the link between them.

"TIME TO GO," a voice said, coming to Nilson Medina from a distance, through the crimson fog that filled his skull like cotton batting.

Did he mutter something in response? Medina wasn't sure and frankly didn't care. The pain was everything, all he could think about, if this could even qualify as thinking. Time to go? Go where? Was it the voice of Death informing him that he had suffered amply for one lifetime, and was now released?

If so, it might be worthwhile to respond.

Medina opened his right eye a little, squinting through a film of blood. His left eye was too swollen to respond. No matter. One eye was enough to recognize the scowling face of his interrogator and bring back the memories of all that he had suffered here—wherever *here* might be.

"You hear me?" asked the leader of the men who'd snatched Medina from his flat hours or eons earlier.

Medina answered, or believed he had, but got a stinging slap as his reward. Compared to the pervasive pain that throbbed and radiated through his body, that blow barely registered.

"You speak when spoken to!" his captor ordered.

But Medina coughed instead, spraying the surly face with bloody phlegm.

He could see the fist draw back, prepare to strike, but someone on the sidelines gripped the rising arm and muttered that the general said no more.

Medina wondered what he'd done to earn the great man's favor, then decided that he didn't care. It hardly mattered now, in any case. If he wasn't already dying from his injuries, Medina knew that they wouldn't release him.

Hurried hands unbound Medina, caught him when he slumped and would have fallen from his chair onto the concrete floor. They got him on his feet and kept him there, though every aching bone and muscle in his body answered to the pull of gravity. Medina's clothes were all in tatters, but they forced his arms into a raincoat's baggy sleeves, then cinched its belt around his waist. Medina thought he had to look like a scarecrow, but there were no mirrors in the warehouse to confirm it for his single blurry eye.

His captors led him toward the exit, nearly dragging him because his legs had turned to rubber, hoisting him across the exit's threshold and propelling him toward one of several waiting cars. No blindfold, which confirmed Medina's first suspicion that he wouldn't be released alive.

And what of that? Did any of it matter now? As best he could recall, Medina hadn't spilled the only secret that his captors seemed concerned about. He hadn't named Matt Cooper, and couldn't have revealed the tall man's whereabouts even if he had been inclined to do so.

It was enough to know that Cooper was still at large, still fighting.

He would make the bastards pay.

"YOU PLAY YOUR CARDS RIGHT," Bolan told Camara, as they rolled northeastward toward the former U.S. embassy, "and you should come out of this thing in decent shape."

"I doubt it," Camara said, sounding glum.

"Consider the alternative," Bolan suggested. "You're still breathing. Count it as a bonus."

"But for how long, eh? Diallo has long arms. He'll stop at nothing to eliminate me when he realizes that I've turned against him."

"How's that any different from him telling me to kill you?" Bolan asked. "He's finished with you, either way. Your job's to get him first, or help the law take care of him."

"The law!" Camara scoffed. "What law? Suppose that he allows himself to be arrested, rather than dispatching troops to overthrow the government. Suppose, also, that the Supreme Court Justices agree to hear his case, and they convict him. What becomes of our Diallo then? Do you think the First Squadron will hold him? That his troops will let him spend a single night in custody?"

"Just take it one step at a time," Bolan suggested. "Tell your story to the captain, listen to his plan, see what he has in mind."

"It all comes out the same," Camara answered. "With my death."

"This deal was your idea," Bolan reminded him. "Remember the alternative."

"Of course. Death now or death tomorrow, possibly next week. I should be thankful, I suppose."

"We've got a saying in the States. Don't look a gift horse in the mouth."

"Gift horse?" Camara wore a puzzled frown.

"Because he might just bite your head off," Bolan finished with a stinger of his own.

"I know you want to kill me," Camara said. "You believe I am an evil man."

"Belief," Bolan replied, "doesn't enter into it. It's not an article of faith for me. You deal in drugs and human misery for profit. If you're not an evil man, who is?"

"The general!" Camara said. "At least I never swore an oath to God and country, as he did. You ask too much of me, a simple man raised in poverty."

"Keep playing that tune," Bolan said. "Maybe, if you can

make it out the other side of this alive, you'll find a new job as a televangelist."

Camara shifted gears and asked, "Will you return the cocaine to Diallo, as you said?"

"I'll play as straight with him," Bolan said, "as he does with me."

"You think he means to cheat you, then?"

"Don't you?"

"Of course," Camara said. "I have no doubt of it."

"Well, there you go."

"What if your friend is still alive?"

"My worry," Bolan said. "Just concentrate on holding up your end of the agreement with the men who plan on keeping you alive."

"I will," the mobster said, "if they can find a court to listen."

"Have a little faith," Bolan told him, hearing it ring hollow even as he spoke the words.

"Ah, faith," Camara said. "The evidence of things not seen. Your Bible."

"Not *my* bible," Bolan answered, "but it gets around."

"I've seen too much of life to trust in gods or live in fear of devils. Men, I find, are bad enough."

"Then work together with the ones who want to help you," Bolan said. "And keep your eyes peeled, now. We're almost there."

13

The former United States embassy in Bissau occupied a corner lot, two blocks south of the capital's central market. Office workers currently occupied the site during business hours, but it remained a landmark of sorts for the few Western tourists who spent time in Guinea-Bissau. Bolan found it easily, reaching the site ahead of time, and boxed the block, scanning for anything that might suggest an ambush.

He found nothing, but consulted his reluctant passenger to be on the safe side. "See anything? It's your life on the line if anybody pulls a fast one."

"Nothing," Camara replied. "You see what I see."

"Okay, then."

Bolan found an empty stretch of curb, southwest of what had once been legally considered U.S. territory, and parked the Peugeot. He killed its engine as he half turned in his seat to face Camara. "It's an easy walk," he said. "No more than half a block, but we're exposed. Wide open. If you bolt, there's no place you can hide."

"I've come this far," Camara said. "Let us complete my degradation."

Bolan left the car first, walked around to get Camara's door and let him out. It was an act of common sense, not chivalry. He didn't plan to give his prisoner a hint of breathing room until he was secure in custody.

And sure, it *was* a short walk, but it felt like miles. The streetlights—those that worked—made Bolan feel that the two of them were sitting ducks. The FAL assault rifle he carried underneath a lightweight raincoat occupied Bolan's right hand. His left hung loose but was prepared at any moment for a snatch and grab, if his companion tried to break away and run for it.

When they were halfway to the former embassy, a man rounded the corner, stopped and watched them drawing closer. He was African, about five-nine and husky, with a gun's bulge beneath the suit jacket he wore unbuttoned. Bolan wished he had a photo of Joseph Mansaré, but he couldn't get one now.

Nothing to do but play it out and hope for the best.

When they were close enough to speak in normal tones, the new arrival said, "I am Captain Mansaré. And you are…?"

"Delivering, as we agreed," Bolan said. "I believe you know Edouard Camara?"

"We have never met," Mansaré said, "but I've been looking forward to this moment."

"I love being popular," Camara stated. His sour face and tone belied his words.

"You will enjoy the grand accommodations I've arranged for you," Mansaré said. And then, to Bolan, "I accept this prisoner—"

The bullet struck Camara just behind and below his right ear, producing hydrostatic shock that pushed the left side of his face completely out of true within a heartbeat, then erupting from his left cheek in a cloud of crimson spray and mutilated tissue. Bolan heard the shot a fraction of a second later, echoing along the street from somewhere at his back, perhaps a hundred yards away.

He didn't have to warn Joseph Mansaré they were under sniper fire. The cop was on his way to cover, lurching toward the former embassy's facade and recessed doorway, clutching at his own face as he ran. Wounded? Bolan glimpsed blood as he was turning, looking for a muzzle flash, not finding it.

He had a choice to make and made it, following Mansaré toward the nearby building in a sprint.

JOSEPH MANSARÉ HUDDLED in the doorway, shielded for the moment by a concrete pillar. Withdrawing his hand from his cheek, where the bullet or something had stung him, he found the palm bloody. A sticky sensation told him there was blood on his forehead, as well, but it wouldn't be his.

"Just a graze," the American said, crouched beside him in deep shadow cast by the nearest streetlight. "The slug or bone fragments. It's bound to get worse if we hang around here."

Mansaré risked a look around the pillar, toward the place where Camara's corpse lay on the sidewalk, a dark pool spreading from his shattered skull. So much for any fantasy he'd cherished of indicting General Diallo and bringing him to trial. That fleeting hope was dead, and Mansaré would be, too, unless he escaped from the trap in short order.

He fumbled for his cell phone, stopped to wipe his blood-slick fingers on his slacks, then tried again. Just as he opened it, the man beside him closed a hand around Mansaré's wrist. "Calling for backup?"

"Should I not?"

"I'd rather you didn't," the American replied, and plucked the phone out of his hand, making it disappear into a pocket.

"What are we to do, then?" Mansaré asked.

"Take a detour, for starters."

As he spoke, the tall man turned and drew a pistol with a sound suppressor attached, stepped to the nearby door and fired a muffled shot into its dead-bolt lock. He pushed it open and stepped across the threshold, pausing as he asked Mansaré, "Are you coming?"

Mansaré followed him reluctantly, drawing his Beretta 92 and feeling better with the weapon in his hand. He didn't reckon that the white man meant him any harm, but neither did Mansaré trust the stranger to protect him absolutely.

Once inside the building, they were faced with choices. Stairs rose on their left and right to reach a mezzanine, while from the lobby where they stood a hallway led straight through to a back door, perhaps one hundred feet away. The corridor was lined with offices on either side.

"Exit," the American said, and set off for the back door, which, Mansaré knew from personal experience, opened onto a parking lot surrounded by an eight-foot wall. He followed, picturing the rolling gate that granted access to the lot from a side street, where he had parked his car.

Easy.

Within two minutes, likely less, they stood at the back door. Mansaré watched as the American unlocked it without peering through its wire-mesh window at the lot outside. Of course, with the lights behind them, nothing could be seen in the darkness. Gunmen could be waiting out there, primed to cut them down.

"I doubt they've got this covered, but you're free to wait around and greet whoever answers the alarm," the American said.

"Alarm?"

"Sure. You saw the tape, right? Silent here, but I imagine that it's ringing off the wall right now at your headquarters."

"Ah."

"Sorry about our deal," the American said.

"Where are you going now?" Mansaré asked.

"First thing, I need to find out if the sniper's waiting. Probably he's gone by now. From here, I still have business with the general."

"He'll kill you," Mansaré said, "as he did Camara."

"If you know that," the American replied, "you know he has a spy among your people. I'd take care of that, if I were you."

And he was gone into the night, a shadow merging with the darkness, lost to sight.

OUTSIDE, BOLAN WAS COVERED by the wall around the parking lot as he turned to his left, or south, back toward the main road. Picking out a spot that should be sheltered by a row of trees from sniper fire, assuming that the shooter had remained in place, he scaled the wall and dropped to a sidewalk on the other side. His Peugeot stood a block away, most of that distance open ground, and there was no way to conceal himself en route.

Just do it, Bolan thought, and stepped from cover, carrying his FAL as he had done before, partly concealed but ready to respond at any sign of opposition. No shots exploded from the darkness, though he would have been an easy target through a scope at any reasonable range. Camara's fatal wound, from what he'd glimpsed of it, suggested that the sniper had been firing from street level, either from the sidewalk or a vehicle. Whichever, he'd have known Mansaré was a cop and clearly hadn't wished to hang around waiting for reinforcements to arrive.

Bolan was at the Peugeot's wheel and pulling out when he heard sirens in the distance, drawing closer by the moment. He then remembered the policeman's cell phone, and pitched it from his open window as he drove, thereby eliminating any prospect of a tail by GPS.

Camara's death was inconvenient for Mansaré, but the odds against successful prosecution of Diallo in his homeland had been astronomical to start with. Perhaps the ambush would convince Mansaré that his own police force needed cleaning up. However that turned out, the mobster's execution put no crimp in Bolan's plans. He hadn't counted on a court to deal with General Diallo—and, in fact, preferred to do the job himself.

He knew now, beyond speculating, that whatever kind of meeting he arranged to swap Nilson Medina for the liberated drugs would be a trap. Diallo literally had an army to command, some forty-five hundred members in all, but some of those were support troops, while others would be scattered nationwide, patrolling borders and pursuing other tasks. With that in mind, before he even set the meet, Bolan began thinking of ways to level out the playing field.

How could eleven hundred pounds of pure Colombian cocaine play into his offensive strategy? For starters, it was too damned much to carry, so he'd have to ditch most of it before going in. Bolan had no compunction about cheating General Diallo, since he'd never planned to give up the coke, in any case. On the other hand, some of it might prove useful as a weapon.

He would need a few things first, additions to his mobile

arsenal, and Bolan knew exactly where to find them. Granted, it was risky going back to shop for more, but no one would expect him, and if he had any trouble with the dealer…well, at this point, what was one more dead offender added to his ever-growing list?

Nothing at all.

NILSON MEDINA FINALLY knew where he was, and it wasn't good. Delivery to army headquarters confirmed that his captors were either regular soldiers or "police" from the Special Intervention Force. In either case, Medina reckoned that he was as good as dead.

And thinking that, he hoped that they would finish with him soon.

Instead, to his surprise, they took him to see General Diallo. Two of his interrogators held Medina upright, more or less, before Diallo's desk. The man who'd been in charge of grilling Medina regretfully explained that they had drawn no useful information from their prisoner, but vowed success if he was only granted further time.

"Forget it," Diallo said. "It no longer matters. I expect to hear from his accomplice soon, with details for exchanging this one."

"An exchange, sir?" the torturer asked. It was his turn to be surprised, apparently, but he stopped short of questioning Diallo's judgment.

"Don't concern yourself with details," the general told him. "Arrangements will be made, delivery accepted, then we'll have the second man as well. I'll let you question him, but if you cannot get results within a reasonable time, I will be forced to call on someone more…experienced."

"We will not fail you, sir," he replied, spreading responsibility among the other members of his crew.

"I hope not, Captain," Diallo said. "But, in any case, I plan to take precautions. We must cancel out this threat tonight. No more delays, no more excuses."

"Sir," the captain—torturer, to Medina—said, "I hope we won't be using any of Camara's men."

"Forget about Camara. He is no longer a matter of concern. In fact, he's history," Diallo said.

Medina would have smiled at that, if he'd been able to control the muscles in his battered, swollen face. Regardless, he was smiling on the inside, knowing that whatever happened next—and he was surely bound to die—at least he had outlived Edouard Camara. Guinea-Bissau would be marginally better off without him, but there was no doubt that General Diallo would replace the mobster with another puppet under his control.

"What should we do with this one while we're waiting, sir?" Captain Torturer asked.

"Clean him up as best you can," Diallo ordered. "I suppose there's little you can do about the injuries."

"A medic, sir?"

"Don't bother. I have never understood the concept of investing time and care in someone you plan to execute."

And there it was, Medina's death sentence pronounced in front of him. It would have been a time to curse and fight, but he had no strength left, couldn't have stood upright without support from those who had abused him, close on either side. If they delayed his execution long enough he might regain some strength, perhaps even discover something he could turn into a weapon, though he doubted that. Diallo and his captain weren't fools.

Medina's only realistic hope, now, was to wait until the meeting General Diallo had described, then use his final ounce of strength, his dying breath, to warn Matt Cooper about the trap. It might already be too late—probably *was,* in fact—but at the very least Medina's death could count for something, even if it proved to be a wasted token gesture.

And who knew? Perhaps Cooper would be lucky. In the time before they killed him, maybe he would put a bullet through Ismael Diallo's brain.

THE DEALER LOOKED SURPRISED when Bolan showed up at his junkyard for the second time. He'd been accommodating to a point, but Bolan caught him fumbling around with something in his pants pocket and called him on it, quickly learning that the older man was trying to dispatch a speed-dial message on his cell phone, but arthritic fingers had delayed him. So he died, and Bolan saved the money he'd allotted for his second spending spree.

He took more rockets for his RPG, then found the item he had seen last time and filed away unconsciously. It was an E1 mortar, copied from venerable British two-inch model used in World War II, produced these days by India's Ordnance Factory Board. It weighed eleven pounds, baseplate included, and could lob its two-pound HE ammo at a rate of twelve rounds per minute if the gunner was in a hurry. Depending on terrain and other circumstances, it could strike a target some 860 yards away.

It was the ammo that concerned Bolan, together with the RPG rounds he was carrying. He'd pondered what to do with all the general's cocaine, and finally decided he should give it back piecemeal. Dismantling and refilling the mortar rounds was a relatively simple job for someone with Bolan's skill as an armorer. Ditto the RPG rounds. It wasn't a perfect delivery system, but it was better than nothing—120 projectiles packed with prime Colombian flake on top of their HE charges.

Call it a smokescreen of a different kind.

He torched the rest of the Bubaque shipment with a dose of gasoline, too much left over for the Peugeot 308 to carry, and he wore the gas mask he had added to his final shopping list while it went up in smoke. The mask was a model made in Israel for civilians, and it seemed to do the trick, no buzz or any other symptoms when the breeze shifted and let the smoke waft over him.

So far, so good.

When he was satisfied that nothing saleable remained, Bolan removed the mask, brushed off his clothes to rid himself of any residue and left the dying fire to burn itself out as the night wore on. He had another call to make, presumably his last, to set the meeting with Diallo for their merchandise exchange. Bolan was counting on a double cross, but hoped that his demand for proof of life had spared Nilson Medina for a few more hours, at least.

If not? Well, he still had Diallo's product to deliver in an unexpected way, and Bolan meant to give the general his due, no matter what. Whether Medina was alive and waiting for him, or already six feet underground, Diallo had a tab to settle with the Executioner. He didn't know it yet, but that bill had come due and Bolan was preparing to collect.

In blood.

"My friend," Ismael Diallo said, forcing a joviality he didn't feel into his voice. "I have what you require."

"So put him on," the caller said.

Only ten minutes had passed since the stranger's last call, asking for the proof that his accomplice was alive, and General Diallo had delayed him, answered honestly enough that he hadn't known when the call would come and needed time to have Nilson Medina brought before him. Now, with the policeman sagging in a chair before his desk, Diallo passed the telephone across.

"Your comrade," Diallo said. "Reassure him that you're still alive, will you?"

Medina took the phone and raised it to one ragged-looking ear, speaking through lips swollen to half again their normal size. "I told them nothing," he announced, without a salutation. Listened briefly, then said, "No, you must not. They—"

Diallo signaled Captain Loua, who immediately snatched the phone away, returned it to the general.

"There," Diallo said. "You're satisfied?"

"So far," the American replied. "Best I can do to match it is a snapshot of your cargo, from my cell phone."

"I'll be pleased to see it, certainly."

"Okay. It's coming through."

Diallo waited for a moment, then beheld a photograph of

bundles wrapped in plastic, keeping the American on hold until he'd counted stacks and multiplied the number in his head. So many, seemingly intact.

"How will you transport them?" Diallo asked, at last.

"My problem," the American replied. "We have a deal, or not?"

"By all means, if you're willing to accommodate my terms for the delivery."

"Let's hear them."

"I require a measure of security, you understand, after the havoc you and Officer Medina have created recently."

"Still listening," the caller said.

"I take for granted that you would not wish to meet at army headquarters?"

"You take it right."

"In which case, I propose a meeting at what you Americans might call my home away from home. There is a camp of sorts outside Ponta Gardete, eight miles southwest of Bissau. I can provide the GPS coordinates if you—"

"I'll find it," said the caller, interrupting him.

Diallo checked his watch and calculated travel time, with necessary preparations at the site, before he said, "Shall we say midnight?"

"Suits me," the American replied. "I'll see you there."

Diallo was about to answer when the dial tone's humming cut him off. A surge of anger welled inside him, but he swallowed it with difficulty, told himself that he would be avenged for every insult soon enough. His first priority was setting up the trap to snare his enemy.

"Put this creature in the car, Captain," he told Loua, with a parting sneer at Nilson Medina. "Then make sure the other troops are ready to depart. We leave in fifteen minutes. Any man not present and accounted for shall spend the next month at hard labor, clearing swampland."

"Yes, sir!" Without waiting for acknowledgment of his salute, Captain Loua snatched Medina from his chair and marched him toward the door. Another moment and it closed behind them, leaving Diallo alone with his thoughts.

He was excited by the prospect of bloodletting, minor as it might turn out to be, but a sensation of anxiety still nagged at Diallo. The man he planned to kill, after thorough interrogation, had already proved himself a ruthless and resourceful bastard. He would kill without remorse to reach his goal, whatever that turned out to be.

Diallo had the same approach to life, which helped explain his worry.

The opponent he would face tonight, he thought, was very like himself.

14

Diallo had given Bolan nearly three hours to travel eight miles, but that didn't prompt Bolan to dawdle. Quite the reverse, in fact, as he considered why the general himself required that time to reach the camp he had described.

To bait a trap, perhaps.

Already halfway there, Bolan maintained a steady sixty miles per hour with the Peugeot 308, clearing a mile a minute with no sign of any traffic cops or other obstacles to slow him. With preparations of his own to make before the showdown, arms and ammunition to be set in place after a recon of the general's facility, he had no time to waste.

A home away from home, my ass, he thought. Unless his educated guess was miles off target, General Diallo would have soldiers waiting at the meeting site and would be bringing reinforcements with him. After the losses he had suffered recently, the army's chief of staff would tolerate no risk of finding himself and his people outgunned.

How many soldiers would he wind up facing? Bolan didn't know and didn't care. He owed Medina this attempt to free him, even if the gutsy little cop was killed as soon as Bolan hung up on Diallo. One way or another, payment would be made.

That left Bolan with a dilemma. If Diallo fielded members of the Special Intervention Force, he would be faced with members of a law enforcement agency who were exempt, as such, from death at Bolan's hands. How would he draw the line when it came down to pulling triggers in the chaos that was combat?

Bolan calculated that his only proper course of action was to mark his targets by their uniforms. Soldiers would turn up in fatigues or something similar, while any plainclothes adversaries would be cops.

How would he deal with them? His private rule on use of deadly force was absolute, but *wounding* was another proposition altogether. In the past, he'd rendered crooked cops unconscious, leaving them to be arrested by their honest brethren, and he'd left a few with flesh wounds. If a killer cop or two got kneecapped in the heat of battle, as he fought to free Nilson Medina, Bolan thought he just might give himself a pass on that.

And if it didn't do the trick, if things came down to do or die, then he would check out with his principles intact.

But he wouldn't be checking out alone.

Unknown to General Diallo, Bolan had the rural compound marked already on his list of targets slated for obliteration if the Guinea-Bissau blitz required it, and he recognized the northbound access road as he approached it, slowing for the turnoff. Rolling on three-quarters of a mile with trees arched overhead, he watched for landmarks he had seen on Google Earth and found the spot he'd chosen in advance, an unpaved track that veered off into trees and undergrowth with room enough to hide his car from passersby.

When he had killed the Peugeot's lights and engine, Bolan exited the car and stripped down, donning his blacksuit and the combat webbing hung with pouches for spare magazines and frag grenades. It would require three trips on foot to fetch the mortar and its special rounds, but Bolan took the RPG and its reloaded rockets with him on his first approach to General Diallo's camp.

He still had ample time to bait a death trap of his own and watch the rats arrive.

For the first time since his kidnapping, Nilson Medina knew where he was going—and, perhaps, where he was meant to die. He drew no personal encouragement from his being still alive. He was a pawn of his abductors', marched out to the vehicle that carried him to meet his fate, alive simply to lure Matt Cooper into position for his own annihilation. In his heart, Medina knew that General Diallo had no plans for either man to see another sunrise. It would be a foolish lapse in judgment.

And whatever else he might be, General Diallo was no fool.

They kept Medina's hands bound, so he had no opportunity to grab a weapon from the gunmen who escorted him. If he was desperate enough, Medina knew that he could kick or head butt them, but to what end? Armed and positioned as they were, they'd simply beat him down—or execute him, if the general allowed it.

Better, he decided, to conserve what strength he still possessed for a more crucial moment, when it might do Cooper some good. If nothing else, Medina thought, there was a chance that he could throw himself in front of guns trained on the man he'd come to think of as an unexpected friend.

And if that failed, perhaps he could get close enough to bite one of his captors on the face—or better yet, his throat—and leave the bastard scarred as a remembrance of this night. A futile gesture, surely, but still better than nothing in the end.

The convoy slowed as they approached Ponta Gardete, and he saw the lead car turn onto the road that would deliver them to General Diallo's compound. Though he'd never visited the site before, Medina knew its layout from aerial photos on file at the Ministry of Justice, now retrievable as if by magic on the internet. Presumably, the web shots had been taken from a satellite in space. Medina didn't understand the new technology, but hoped his knowledge of the camp might help him—or help Cooper—when the inevitable killing started.

If he had been religious, Medina thought, this would be the time for him to pray. But as it was, he only had his bruised self-confidence and Cooper's ability to overcome imposing odds. Neither, he feared, would be enough to see them through the next few hours alive, but at the very least their enemies would suffer in the act of killing them, and know they had been in a bitter fight.

Sometimes that was the best a man could do.

After a mile of following the access road, shocks jolting over potholes all the way, the convoy slowed for its approach to the guarded gates. Medina, wedged between his keepers, saw one of the sentries peer into Diallo's car, then snap off a salute before he barked an order at his two companions. Moments later, with the gate now rolled aside, the caravan rolled through and circled toward that portion of the camp where vehicles were lined up side by side. A motor pool of sorts, with more soldiers on guard.

"Get out," Captain Torturer told him, when their car was parked, its engine silent. "Stretch your legs while you still can."

CAPTAIN ABDOUL LOUA shoved his prisoner into the shed they'd set aside for his confinement, its lone piece of furniture a plastic bucket for collecting waste material, superfluous unless his hands were freed. Nilson Medina stumbled, almost falling, then turned back to face the doorway after he regained his balance.

"Not first-class accommodation, I'm afraid," Loua said. "But it should be good enough for your remaining time."

"How long is that?" Medina asked him, lisping slightly with his swollen lips and bitten tongue.

"Your friend has an appointment with the general at midnight," Loua answered, glancing at his watch. "If he's on time, you have about two hours and twenty minutes left."

"Why don't we spend it in a friendly competition?" Medina asked. "Free my hands and leave your guns outside."

"It's tempting," Loua granted, "but I doubt that it would be much of a contest in your present state."

"I see. You only face opponents when they're duct-taped to a chair," Medina said.

Loua suppressed the flash of anger, forced a smile and said, "We'll see when I bring you the white man's head. Five minutes after midnight, shall we say?"

Medina laughed, then spit onto the dirt floor of his cell. "Goodbye, Captain," he said.

Loua backed out, padlocked the door and moved off to inspect the camp's perimeter. There was chain-link fencing topped with coils of razor wire on every side, but it wasn't electrified, and in the absence of alarms he knew the wire could easily be cut. Not trusting General Diallo's regulars to check it properly, he set off on his own to walk the fence and verify that it was still intact.

The hike would also give him time to think.

Loua was angry at himself for being goaded by Medina. The pathetic prisoner was nearly dead, yet he had gotten under Loua's skin and come close to provoking an assault that might have finished him. Was that his game, in fact? Knowing that he was doomed, had he set out to sabotage the fraudulent exchange to liberate the general's cocaine? After the ordeal he had suffered, could Medina even think that clearly?

And he seemed to have such confidence in the American he'd only known for…what? Less than two days. As if the white man was some kind of superhero who could swoop down from the sky and save Medina from the fate that had been planned for him. Ridiculous! One man against an army was no contest, even if Diallo's regulars were lazy, poorly trained and sometimes insubordinate.

The odds were all against the American. There was no hope that he could survive.

Especially if Loua found him first.

"I welcome it," he muttered to himself, passing a sentry on the fence line.

When the private turned to blink at him, Loua snapped, "Watch the forest, idiot!" and left a newly minted enemy scowling behind him.

Damn Medina for suggesting that he feared the white man! Nothing could be further from the truth. Loua had never run from any fight, and while he'd lost a few in childhood, that was long ago.

"I welcome it!" he said again. And dared the night to prove him wrong.

BOLAN SURVEYED THE COMPOUND, picking out its obvious command post and communications shack, two Quonset huts, the motor pool, mess hall, latrine, three rows of two-man tents, the metal shed that held Nilson Medina under lock and key.

He'd watched Diallo move about the camp, directing junior officers while Bolan counted heads and took stock of the enemy. Three dozen tents for privates gave him thirty-six, while officers and noncoms occupied the prefab huts. Diallo would have bedded down in the CP if there'd been time to spare, but this would be a busy night and Bolan didn't see him getting any sleep.

Until the big one.

Bolan's vantage point was a ridge overlooking the camp two hundred yards out, screened by forest from direct line of sight. He'd worked out the distance while waiting for Diallo's men to settle in, then backed off to the high ground where the E1 mortar stood with shells laid out around it, ready to fly. The RPG and its rockets were stashed in the woods, closer in, where Bolan could retrieve them on his way to penetrate the compound.

First things first, and that meant waiting.

Not that Bolan planned to keep his midnight date with General Diallo. Not exactly. Strolling to the gate for any kind of face-to-face was tantamount to suicide. Diallo wanted to retrieve his stolen cargo, sure, but he'd also take for granted that Medina's ally was a solo act, with no risk in grabbing him besides a loss of soldiers when they swarmed him. Later, as the general would reason, there'd be time enough to learn where the cocaine was stashed, while they were grilling him to death.

No, thanks.

Bolan had a very different scenario in mind. He wasn't sure that he could extricate Medina from the camp alive, but there was absolutely no hope if he blundered down to meet the enemy and wound up in a cage himself. His plan was rash, audacious, but at least it offered *some* hope for Medina.

Call it one in twenty, maybe twenty-five.

Better than nothing, anyway.

He'd registered the small shed where Medina was confined, well separated from the CP, motor pool and other targets plotted on the map in Bolan's head. Controlling shrapnel was impossible, but he could definitely shell the compound without scoring a direct hit on the prison hut. If their positions were reversed, Bolan knew he would give the go-ahead. He hoped Medina would have felt the same, considering the grim alternative, but had to play his hand without approval from his incapacitated partner.

Overhead, a half moon lit the forest treetops, beaming down on Bolan's firebase. It reminded him of other jungle nights, when he had waited for the action to begin, his fate to be decided in a contest of his own ability against the enemy's. So far, the Executioner had always walked away and left his adversaries on the battlefield.

His luck had held.

And this time? There was no way to predict the outcome, but he came to every fight with reasoned confidence in his ability and preparation. Beyond that, it all came down to guts and luck.

Another soldier might have prayed for help, an unseen hand to guide his own and tweak his aim, but Bolan was averse to off-loading responsibility. Whatever happened in the next half hour or so, he would be shouldering the credit—or the blame—himself. No crying afterward that unseen deities had failed him by ignoring his entreaties.

This part, every soldier had to do alone.

And live or die with how the hand played out.

ONE HOUR, GENERAL DIALLO THOUGHT, checking his watch by moonlight. There were spotlights stationed here and there around the camp, facing the forest, but he'd ordered them switched off. Inside the compound, likewise, he had doused most of the lights, aside from one in his command post, one inside the mess hall and a third by the latrine. The last thing that he needed, at the moment, was some clumsy private falling in a slit trench, floundering in muck.

One hour, and Diallo knew his adversary had to be close by now, if he was coming. There had always been a chance that the American would try to dupe him, set the time for an exchange of drugs for his associate, then strike somewhere in Bissau while Diallo and his soldiers were away. A possibility, but he believed the white man would appear on schedule, compelled by some archaic sense of honor, duty, call it what you like.

The cocaine worried him, of course. It would require a dozen of his strongest men to shift that load by hand, and driving it up to the gates of his camp would be madness. No, he thought his enemy would likely bring a sample with him, probably one kilo, seeking to exchange directions to the rest for what was left of his accomplice. It was logical—and it would also be his last mistake.

Diallo had a squad of soldiers hidden in the woods, outside the wire, prepared to move in on his signal, cutting off the fool American's retreat when he arrived, most probably on foot. That team was scattered, since Diallo realized his adversary might not come directly to the camp's gate, but their focus was the access road that linked his compound to the outside world. Between them and rest of his defenders, led by Captain Loua's small detachment from the Special Intervention Force, Diallo had no fear that he would let the white man slip away.

Not this time.

His mistake during the previous attacks had been trusting Edouard Camara to resolve the problem. Certainly Camara—may he rot in peace—had copious experience in dealing with and killing off assorted felons like himself, but when he'd faced a soldier in the field, he'd proved completely useless. Under other circumstances, General Diallo might have thanked the white man for exposing Camara's ineptitude, but thanks would play no part in their dialogue later this night.

There would be questions, screaming—and, perhaps, some valuable answers.

And if, at last, his enemy refused to speak in spite of all Diallo's efforts, killing him by inches, slowly, would be its own reward. Let his fate serve as an example to all future challengers, a lesson etched in blood.

The crisis that had challenged General Diallo would become a triumph when his enemies were crushed, the news of their demise broadcast through sources he could trust. He would emerge a stronger man, whose future enemies would think more carefully before attacking him.

And those who dared, in spite of everything, would surely die.

NILSON MEDINA STRAINED against the plastic ties that bound his wrists behind his back, but only felt them biting deeper into his bruised and bloodied flesh. Police loved them for binding suspects, since the ties couldn't be loosened, only cut, and there was no lock to be picked as in the case of handcuffs. Finally, disgusted, he admitted to himself that he couldn't fight with his hands.

That left his feet, his knees, his teeth, whatever else Medina could employ against his captors when they came for him next time. Escape remained a fantasy, but one good kick to the captain's balls would improve Medina's mood immensely. Nothing that might happen after that held any interest for him, since he knew he was as good as dead.

And what of it?

This was a logical result of his decision to collaborate with Matt Cooper in a two-man war against Camara's network and the army that supported it. Medina, at some level, knew that victory was hopeless. Had he simply reached a point in life where he had seen too much corruption and no longer cared what happened next? All that mattered was if he could strike a passing blow against the blight that stained his homeland's honor. What had he achieved, in fact?

Nothing, perhaps—except to some extent the recovery of his diminished pride. And given what awaited him tonight, he would make do with that.

But his torturer…

If Medina saw a chance to sink his teeth into the captain's throat, how sweet the blood from his carotid artery would taste. Now *that* would be a fitting final meal before his execution. Sadly, he reckoned that the prospect was a fantasy.

How long remaining now, before Cooper kept his rendezvous with General Diallo? Did he have some trick in mind, to shift the odds he faced? If they'd been able to communicate, Medina would have told Cooper to move on, forget about him and destroy the drugs they'd stolen from Camara. He could always try to kill the general another time, perhaps from ambush with a sniper's rifle or the RPG.

It seemed a bitter waste for the American to sacrifice himself this way, when he had to know Medina's time was nearly up. They might be comrades for the moment, but they weren't relatives or lifelong friends. Their brief relationship, contrived by circumstance, demanded no self-sacrifice.

Medina wondered what he would have done for Cooper if their situations were reversed. Might he have risked his life one final time, certain of losing it, for someone he had known for barely two days' time? What was the point?

Simply to be a man, perhaps. To keep his word and honor a friendship forged in battle.

Knowing that he would be responsible for Cooper's death, and would end forever any hope of the American combating evil on some other front, Medina's disappointment with himself increased. Whatever he'd accomplished since he joined forces with Cooper, he was a failure in the end.

Tears stung his one good eye and spilled over his cheek. Medina cursed his weakness—but his muttered words were lost as an explosion rocked Diallo's camp.

15

Bolan dropped a second round into the E1 mortar, turned his face away and heard the *pong* sound as it launched, two more rounds ready in his hands. He figured four on one mark ought to get the party started, then he'd make adjustments as he went, marching a storm of high-explosive charges packed with pure cocaine across the length and breadth of General Diallo's camp.

How much coke would survive each blast? He didn't have a clue, but there should be enough flake mingled with the drifting smoke and dust down there to make his adversaries fuzzy-headed, at the very least. Toss in the shock waves and the flying shrapnel from successive shell bursts, and he had a fairly decent recipe for hell on earth.

Just what the doctor ordered for a general who'd run amok.

Nilson Medina would be in the middle of it, but protected somewhat by the prefab building that confined him if he hugged the deck. Bolan could do no more to help him at the moment, though he still clung to a slim hope that he might extract Medina once he got inside the compound. If he got inside.

Big *if*, and very premature.

With two more mortar rounds airborne, Bolan shifted the stovepipe weapon four degrees to starboard, braced it and grabbed two more rounds from the ranks on his left. Although mortars weren't conventional firearms per se, their barrels still heated up during protracted firing. It was Bolan's job, as gunner, to let the weapon cool a bit between four-minute salvos of eight rounds per minute, meaning that with downtime, his hundred hand-packed rounds should be expended within twenty-odd minutes.

A lifetime for many downrange—and time enough, perhaps, for General Diallo's spotters to determine his location, if they kept their wits about them under fire.

No problem.

By the time his last shell left the mortar's smoking tube, Bolan would be in motion, racing down the wooded hillside to retrieve his RPG and launch the second phase of his assault. How many of the hostiles would be down and out by then?

Enough, perhaps.

Besides the explosions downrange, he now heard screams and furious shouting. Diallo's soldiers likely hadn't known what to expect when they were rounded up for duty here. If any of the troops on hand were veterans of Guinea-Bissau's civil war, the shelling might revive old memories, but no one who'd enlisted since the 1999 cease-fire would have been under fire by mortars. He heard panic in the camp, and knew that it could work for him when he went down to find the general.

Time for another pause, Bolan wearing a pair of work gloves as he moved the stovepipe once again, targeting new coordinates. His next rounds would be lofted toward the compound's motor pool, depriving panicked soldiers of escape by any means but running for their lives. If he could detonate the fuel tanks of their cars and trucks, so much the better, spreading chaos and the stench of burning fuel along with drifting clouds of smoke and powder.

He had another twist in mind for the Diallo team, but wasn't activating it until his mortar rounds were nearly spent, when he was ready to approach the camp on foot. Whether it would assist him or rebound disastrously was anybody's guess, but Bolan felt obliged to try it anyway.

The Executioner was pulling out all stops against an army, wondering if it would be his last go-round.

And he was living large—like every other day.

THE DETONATION OF ANOTHER mortar shell—was it the eighth or ninth, so far?—knocked General Diallo sprawling with its shock wave. Cursing, lurching to his feet once more, he felt a wetness on the inside of his thigh and feared he might have soiled himself, then was relieved to see a crimson stain instead. No blood was jetting from the wound, so his femoral artery hadn't been sliced, and he could still walk well enough despite sharp stabs of pain.

It was better than crawling, when his troops were running aimlessly about the camp, squealing like children, others stretched out on the ground wounded or dead. If their commander crumpled, how could they recover from the first shock of bombardment to redeem themselves? More to the point, how would Diallo himself manage to escape?

The damned American had tricked him after all. Weighing the odds, he had decided not to face Diallo like a man, but rather hang back at a distance, wreaking havoc on the compound where Diallo's soldiers couldn't reach him with their small-arms fire.

Another mortar shell exploded in the camp, this one between two trucks parked in the motor pool. A storm of shrapnel ripped through both, and one truck's fuel tank detonated in a ball of oily fire that lit the night. A man caught in the blast went reeling toward the fence line, swathed in flames and screaming on his jerky run to nowhere.

Choking on a cloud of smoke and dust that drifted over him, Diallo noted that his head was swimming, as if he'd drunk too much coca-leaf liqueur. Smoke inhalation might have that effect, he thought, and coughed to clear his lungs. It helped a little, but Diallo stopped when something else distracted him. Oddly enough, the leg wound seemed to pain him less the more he walked on it, so he kept moving, shouting at his frightened men to rally.

And all the while, the shells kept falling, ripping through his trucks and staff cars, shattering their bodies, twisting frames, spreading a lake of burning fuel that lit the camp nearly as bright as day. Diallo viewed the wreckage, understanding that their only hope of getting out now was to kill the man responsible for all that havoc, to erase him from existence as if he'd never been born.

"To me, men! All of you, to me!" he bellowed, moving through the heady haze.

ABDOUL LOUA DUCKED AND DODGED his way across the compound, covering his nose and mouth with one hand as he ran through swirls of battle mist, feeling peculiarly light-headed and yet oddly energized, somehow. He'd been awake for nearly twenty hours, first tracking and capturing Medina, then securing him for Diallo and delivering him to the general's forest camp, but now he seemed to be escaping the fatigue.

If only he could keep his eyes in proper focus, stop their random blurring.

Never mind. He had the prison shed fixed in his sights, no more than fifty yards ahead of him. The guard he'd left outside its padlocked door was gone, most likely frightened by the shelling, but Loua could deal with him later, assuming the negligent soldier survived. First, though, he needed to release the hostage and employ him in a bid to halt his friend's bombardment of the camp.

For who else could it be, lobbing those mortar shells? An army weapon used against the army, and Medina's cohort had already proved himself a more-than-able soldier. Somewhere in the days ahead, Loua would find the dealer who'd supplied him with the mortar. Possibly he'd taken it during the raid on Edouard Camara's private arsenal, but Loua didn't care about the weapon's source just now. He had to stop the damned incessant march of high-explosive shells around the camp, while there were any soldiers left inside with wits and will enough to fight.

He reached the shed and pulled a key ring from his pocket, found it strangely cumbersome and awkward as he grappled with the padlock. Three tries got it done, by which time Loua had begun to curse his hands for joining in the plot against him. Finally, he tossed the lock aside, opened the corrugated metal door and stepped into the shed.

At a glance, it seemed to be empty. For a heartbeat, Loua thought his prisoner had fled, but then Medina charged him from his left, a corner that he would have checked immediately if his brain was functioning at full capacity, propelling Loua to his right, against the nearest wall. The shed vibrated from their impact, but its rattling noise was lost as new explosions rocked the camp.

Medina kicked at Loua, aiming for his groin, but Loua turned in time to save his future progeny and took it on the hip, then lashed back with his automatic rifle, hammering Medina's face. The battered officer collapsed, lay moaning in the dirt while Loua kicked him twice, trying to crack his ribs, rewarded by dull grunting sounds of pain.

Submission, finally.

Cursing Medina and his ancestors, Loua reached down and hauled the stunned policeman to his feet, propelled him through the hut's exit and out into the thunderous night. "Your friend's come calling, Nilson. Do you hear him? Are you idiot enough to think that he can save you?

Half-turned toward him with a bloody grin, Medina said, "Not save me. Just kill you."

"We'll see who gets killed," Loua raged. "If your boyfriend keeps firing, you're next on the slab."

"Let it be, then!" Medina replied with a wild whoop of laughter. "As long as you die at my side."

BOLAN DROPPED HIS LAST two rounds into the E1 mortar, one behind the other in a rapid-fire sequence, and sent them arcing over treetops before plummeting to detonate in General Diallo's camp. The compound's motor pool was burning fiercely, lighting up the sky before him like a small town in the middle distance. Bolan sniffed the breeze and caught the faintest tang of fuel in flames.

Round one was finished. While survivors in the compound scrambled to right fires, collect their wits and rally to defend their site, Bolan reached out for his sat phone, tapping out a number from his memory.

The voice that answered was familiar to him now. Without preamble, Bolan asked, "You know Diallo's country place outside Ponta Gardete?"

"I know where it is," Mansaré answered.

"If you want to see some action, drop on by. They're having fireworks, and you might find somebody you know."

"Medina?"

"One way or another," Bolan said. "It may not be too late."

"I don't have men enough to fight the army," Mansaré said bitterly.

"There shouldn't be too many of them left," Bolan said, then he cut the link.

He left the mortar standing where it was, no danger now that it had sent its last round lofting toward Diallo's forest hideaway. Bolan retrieved his FAL assault rifle and left the high ground, slide-stepping down the west slope of the ridge toward the tree line below him. Firelight was his guide now as he made his way through clingy undergrowth to reach the forward spot where he'd stashed his RPG-7 and cache of rockets.

Diallo's troops had suffered through one taste of hell. They had another coming, and the Executioner wanted this one to be up close and personal.

In fact, the launcher could have reached Diallo's camp from where he'd been, atop the ridge, except for trees that blocked his line of fire downhill. Phase two of Bolan's strike was riskier, in that the RPG's back-blast would make him visible to soldiers in the target zone, inviting hostile fire. Bolan would have to duck and run while he completed his dismantling of the compound, all the while keeping an eye out for Medina in the midst of chaos.

Simple, right. Like falling in an open grave.

He found the spot that he was looking for and slung his rifle, hoisted two fat satchels bristling with rockets that weighed nearly five pounds apiece. Say a hundred pounds even, before he lifted the fifteen-pound launcher and struck off again toward the camp.

Boot camp and Special Forces training had conditioned

Bolan to living, working and fighting in conditions that would have made most men collapse. His life since the army, including a daily exercise routine during his "down" time, had kept him in top fighting form. Still, to slog through an African forest while laden with hardware was taxing, straps chafing his flesh, muscles aching from strain, his lungs fighting for each humid breath.

Never easy, but worth it. That was, if he won.

And behind it was the knowledge that *winning* was never a permanent thing. Every battle would be fought again and again, for as long as he lived. New terrain, perhaps. New faces on the enemy, maybe some variation in their motives.

But it all came down to mud and blood and guts, survival instinct taking over in the crunch.

The best man might not win, but he would damn sure do his best.

CAPTAIN MANSARÉ KNEW he was embarking on a fool's errand— a suicide mission, perhaps—but he couldn't stand idly by while another of his men was murdered by the same men who had dragged his homeland's reputation through the muck of narco-trafficking. For years, he'd told himself that there was nothing to be done. Now, with a glimpse of *something* forced upon him, it would mean the death of soul and self to close his eyes and turn away.

Mansaré's choice, but he wouldn't compel his officers to share the risk against their will. Accordingly, he wasted precious time explaining what had happened—what *was* happening, that very moment, less than ten miles from their headquarters—and called for volunteers.

Of eighteen men on hand, only one slacker shook his head and left the rest, walking slump-shouldered under their collective glare of raw contempt. The rest rushed to the armory, retrieving automatic weapons that they rarely used, stuffing their pockets full of extra magazines.

Arming for war.

How many of them would return alive? Mansaré's phantom

caller had seemed confident that they would face no major opposition, but was he correct? Would he be dead before their convoy reached the camp outside Ponta Gardete? Was he even there, or was his last call some kind of elaborate trick designed to spark a battle to the death between Diallo's soldiers and the Judicial Police?

No, Mansaré thought. Whatever the American had in mind, he had worked with Nilson Medina and had shown no hostility toward other members of the force. If not a friend, precisely, at least he seemed to be an ally of officers sickened by crime and corruption. Cleaning up the city—much less Guinea-Bissau—might be a futile endeavor, but what good were they to anyone if they never even tried?

When his men were armed, Mansaré led them to the motor pool. Eighteen men, including Mansaré, packed themselves into three Land Rover Defenders and rolled out of the ministry's fenced parking lot with a snarling of 2.5-liter I4 turbo diesel engines. The captain double-checked his AK-47, making sure its magazine was seated properly and that he had a live round in the chamber, with the safety on. His sidearm was a Czech-made CZ 75, with twenty 9 mm Parabellum bullets in its magazine.

Mansaré hoped that it would be enough.

BOLAN REACHED THE TREE LINE twenty yards from Diallo's command post, noting shrapnel damage to the prefab building from the mortar rounds. Smoke from the compound wafted his way on a vagrant breeze, and Bolan took time to slip on his gas mask, adjusting the straps that held it in place for an airtight fit. The goggle lenses made it slightly awkward to aim through the RPG's UP-7V telescopic sight, but he managed, fixing its red dot on the south wall of the CP.

The HEAT round struck home, pierced the thin metal wall, then detonated into smoky thunder. Bolan had a second rocket loaded by the time the CP's roof took flight, hoping the compound's occupants were too disorganized and frightened to mark his first back-flash. That wouldn't last long, though, and while he had a bit of breathing room, he sighted on the only truck still standing in one piece, at the far end of the motor pool.

Round two punched through the truck's grille, detonating when it hit the engine block, and knocked the truck off-kilter; oily smoke and drugged fumes roiled from beneath the peeled-back hood. The fuel tank blew a moment later, by which time the Executioner was up and running with his slightly lighter burden, sprinting thirty yards along the camp's perimeter before he stopped to aim and fire again.

Round three scorched through the flimsy chain-link fence to strike the communications hut—again, already damaged—and complete the devastation started by his mortar rounds. This time, he didn't risk a second shot before he rose and ran, backtracking toward the compound's gate. The longer he could keep his adversaries guessing about when and where he'd strike from next, the better chance he had of winnowing the odds and coming out the other side of it alive.

He had the launcher on his shoulder, round four heavy in the tube, when Bolan heard a voice raised from the camp. This one was calling out to him, without a name.

"American!" it shouted. "Do you want your friend?"

It took five seconds to locate the voice's source, a plainclothes gunman moving toward the gate in lockstep with a slouched and limping human shield. Most of the shooter's face was hidden by the man in front of him, whom Bolan recognized at once, despite his injuries.

Nilson Medina. Badly hurt, yet still alive.

But for how long?

"American!" the gunman called again. "I know you hear me! Do you want your friend to live? You made a bargain with the general, and now you've broken it!"

Street clothes told him the hostage-taker was a member of the Special Intervention Force. A cop, at least by virtue of his creds. As such, he was immune to deadly force at Bolan's hands.

But not untouchable.

In fact, the way he acted, Bolan thought he'd already been

touched by one or more of Bolan's "special" mortar rounds. How high he was remained impossible to quantify at this range, and it only mattered insofar as it affected his reaction time and volatility. Would the cocaine he'd snorted without knowing it make him more or less likely to blow out Medina's brains?

Trading his launcher for the FAL, Bolan decided there was only one way to find out.

16

General Diallo saw Abdoul Loua crossing the compound with Nilson Medina, marching the prisoner toward the compound's gate. Loua's movements seemed jerky, but Diallo couldn't tell if the captain was walking with a peculiar gait, or if Diallo's own eyes were playing tricks on him. He still felt dizzy, and there was a buzzing in his ears that didn't sound or feel like a reaction to explosive charges detonating.

The explosions! Suddenly it struck Diallo that they'd stopped. The mortar rounds, then hurtling rockets, were followed by a deathly stillness. The general should have felt relieved, but didn't trust the silence after so much thunder hurled his way. If the American had ceased firing, there had to be a reason for it, and Diallo knew his men hadn't eliminated their opponent. He was out there, somewhere, and no doubt preparing for another strike.

"Captain!" Diallo called to Loua in the relative quiet, nothing but the moans and curses of his wounded to compete with his shout for attention. "Where are you taking that man?"

Loua ignored him—or, to be fair, may have been deafened by close-range explosions. Instantly angry, but willing to grant the benefit of a doubt, Diallo started after Loua, trailed by half a dozen soldiers he had rallied while the mortar blasts were marching back and forth across his compound. If the captain thought that he was leaving with Diallo's prisoner, he had to have lost his mind.

Shell-shocked, perhaps.

Diallo was barely ten paces behind the two men when Loua's right knee buckled, spraying crimson mist. As he was crumpling to the ground, Diallo's buzzing ears picked out a rifle shot, fired somewhere in the dark woods out beyond the chain-link fence and razor wire.

The captain howled in pain, spraying the trees with automatic fire, one-handed, doing no more good than any of Diallo's other soldiers had so far. While he was thus engaged, the general ran forward, scuttling in a crouch, and caught the prisoner. Whipping a meaty arm around Medina's neck, keeping his own head down, Diallo gripped the hostage as a human shield and cried out to the forest, "You have cheated me! We had a bargain!"

In his grip, the bloodied officer surprised Diallo with a cackling laugh. "A bargain!" he crowed. "You try to make a deal with death?"

"Shut up, idiot!" snapped the army's chief of staff.

Then, to the night he called, "You want your friend alive? Why should I give him to you now?"

Another rifle shot rang out. Diallo flinched, but he wasn't the target. To his left, one of his soldiers grunted and collapsed, half of his face a mutilated ruin. Instantly, another shot, this one drilling a trooper on Diallo's right, as he was turning, poised to run.

"Retreat!" Diallo snapped at his surviving troopers, lurching backward from the gate.

And in his dizzy mind, a question formed. Retreat to where?

BOLAN TRACKED THE retreating party, catching glimpses of Diallo's head behind Nilson Medina's bloody and disfigured face, but couldn't hold the vision long enough to risk a shot. Instead, he swung off to the left once more and dropped a third of the original half dozen men Diallo had brought with him to the gate. A puff of scarlet from the soldier's tunic, seen by firelight, and he dropped.

Swing right again, to number four. The trooper fired a long burst from his AK-47, well within killing range if he had fixed on a target, but wasting his rounds as it was. Bolan stroked the FAL's trigger again, punched a hole through the scared soldier's forehead, and watched him go down.

"Não atirem! Eu vou matá-lo!" Diallo shouted, sounding frantic, then apparently recalled who he was talking to, repeating it in English. "Hold your fire! I'll kill him!"

Bolan saw the pistol wedged into Medina's ear, no clear view of Diallo as he weighed the odds. Medina seemed to find him in the darkness with his one good eye, lips twisting in a kind of smile as he called out, "Forget about me! Kill him!"

Diallo struck his captive with the pistol, ducking at the same instant to keep himself hidden, crab-walking Medina to his right rear, farther back into the camp's smoky ruin. As he went, Diallo shouted to his men in Portuguese, bringing the stragglers out to join him, closing ranks around their leader to obscure him.

Bolan set down his rifle, retrieved the RPG and shouldered it. He didn't want to harm Medina, but he had to spook Diallo's men in order to secure a clean shot at the general. If nothing else, he hoped a near miss from a rocket might be adequate to scatter them and buy him time to make that shot. It was a gamble, but it seemed to be his only chance.

He aimed directly at the shuffling clutch of soldiers, then lifted his sights to send the rocket hurtling over their collective heads, just high enough to scorch their hair in passing. Bolan squeezed the launcher's trigger, felt it shudder and saw the fiery tail streak off down range. Diallo's frightened men ducked, breaking off to either side before it reached them and kept going, roaring off into the fiery wreckage of the compound's motor pool.

Bolan exchanged the launcher for his rifle, scanned the battlefield to find Diallo crouching with Medina clutched in front of him. There was a shoulder he could zero in on, with a little luck, if he was quick enough and—

Headlights flared behind him, lighting up the battleground as three black SUVs arrived to join the party. Bolan hesitated for a heartbeat, glancing back to see who was arriving, hoping it would be Joseph Mansaré's men, and when he turned back toward Diallo he had lost his shot.

The general was gone, Medina with him, lost in swirling smoke.

MEDINA FELT AS IF the arm around his neck was strangling him. He gagged, fighting for breath, but his bound hands prevented any effective struggle. He had hoped for sweet oblivion when the rocket sped toward them, but it was a miss. Now, with headlights nearly blinding him, Medina guessed the general had summoned reinforcements to the compound somehow, fielding them against Matt Cooper.

All lost. Their effort wasted.

Furious, he cursed and kicked and squirmed, and was rewarded with a stunning crack across the skull. Diallo kept backpedaling, half dragging and half carrying Medina, clearly still afraid of being shot as he retreated. Wishing Cooper had fired through him to kill the general, Medina felt the burn of futile tears beneath his swollen eyelids, sobbing in frustration as he lurched and scuffed along.

Across the camp, Medina saw the lead car of the new arrivals race forward and smash into the gate. The chain-link bowed, stretching on impact, then the gate's frame tore free of its runners with a harsh metallic squeal and buckled inward, dragging claws along the full length of the steadily encroaching vehicle. Paint scarred from grille to tailgate, the Land Rover bulled its way inside and left the gate a flaccid dangling thing, no obstacle for two more SUVs that rattled over it.

Odd that Diallo's men wouldn't open the gate for their potential rescuers, Medina thought, but they were likely so unnerved by Cooper's relentless shelling that they didn't even realize salvation was at hand. Three vehicles, say fifteen men at least inside them, and the odds were getting worse with every breath Medina took.

He wished that Cooper would cut and run, abandon him and flee while there was time. Live on to fight another day and learn from this experience for future confrontations with a world of enemies. He couldn't save Medina. Guinea-Bissau was a hopeless case.

But something told him the American wouldn't desert him. Not yet, even though it was the wisest thing to do. Cooper had a sense of honor that would get him killed this night, unless Medina helped to change his mind.

Roaring, Medina twisted in his captor's grasp, ignoring blows across his scalp, struggling until he faced the general, then lunged at him, teeth snapping at Diallo's face. They were the only weapon he had left, reverting to primeval savagery. Diallo yelped, recoiling, shoved Medina back with one hand while his other raised the pistol.

Snarling like a rabid thing, Medina saw the muzzle flash, before his world went black.

CAPTAIN MANSARÉ LEAPED from his Land Rover and hit the ground running, conscious of officers following closely. He was on uneasy ground here, physically confronting soldiers with drawn weapons, but the explosions and gunfire he'd witnessed clearly granted any law enforcement officer leave to intervene. Pair that with his suspicion that one of his people was caged in the camp, and Mansaré was prepared to defend his approach before any tribunal.

Whatever happened next would be up to Diallo's men, if any were prepared to challenge him. So far, he'd seen a number of them clearly dead and wounded, scattered here and there around the compound. Others scuttled to and fro, alone or in small groups, firing their weapons toward the forest that surrounded them. So far, few of them seemed to take much notice of the new arrivals on the scene.

Mansaré stopped one running trooper, clutching his arm, and demanded, "What's happening here?"

The young man blinked at him, wild-eyed but rational enough to note the captain's stars on Mansaré's collar. "Shelling, sir," he answered, in a shaky voice. "Rockets. I don't—"

More gunfire crackled from the far side of the camp, and the private twisted loose from Mansaré's grasp, sprinting for the exit created when their Land Rovers had flattened the gate. Mansaré felt his people watching him, swallowed his trepidation as he ordered, "Come with me. We need to find Diallo."

He didn't use the general's rank when he spoke, since Mansaré was prepared to treat Diallo as a criminal, make an arrest on his own authority and face the consequences if his superiors balked. And if the army's chief of staff resisted...?

It was why they'd brought so many weapons, after all.

Mansaré hardly recognized Diallo's compound from the aerial photos on file at his office. Every major building had been damaged or demolished by explosions, and many of the tents were torn by shrapnel. Smoke and haze hung over everything, a smell of burning flesh and gasoline with—what else was it? Not a smell, so much as a *sensation,* tingling in his nostrils.

As if on cue, one of his men sneezed loudly, making several of the others jump. Nobody laughed, under the circumstances, cutting angry glances toward the one who'd made the noise. Mansaré let it go, pressed on across the killing ground, alert for any sign of Diallo or Nilson Medina. The first man that he recognized was hobbling toward them, dragging one bloody leg, face contorted in pain.

Abdoul Loua, captain of the Special Intervention Force.

Before Mansaré had a chance to speak, Loua began to shout at him. "Your little bastard caused all this! Where is he? Give him to me, damn you!"

Mansaré saw the automatic rifle dangling from Loua's right hand and leveled his own weapon, calling out, "Stop where you are! Drop the weapon!"

"All your fault!" Loua said. "We should have wiped you out to start with!"

Loua began to raise his rifle, but Mansaré didn't give him time to fire. A short burst from his AK-47 ripped across the rogue cop's chest, then several of his men were firing, too, their bullets making Loua dance and spin before he dropped, twitched once and then lay still.

Shaking, Mansaré told his people, "Hurry! Find Diallo and Medina. No one stops us now."

BOLAN SAW MOST OF IT from his place outside the wire. Land Rovers rolling in, charging the gate and bashing through it, the policemen piling out. Across the compound, veiled in smoke but visible by firelight, General Diallo grappling with Medina, dragging him until the hostage turned on him and fought, despite bound hands. A close-range pistol shot, Medina falling lifeless. Bolan had Diallo in his sights until a burst of wild fire from the camp swept over him, scoring the trees that sheltered him and causing him to flinch.

When he looked back again, the general was gone.

He scanned the camp, seeking Diallo in the murk and battle smoke, not finding him. The officers who'd plowed in through the gate could be distinguished by their uniforms from General Diallo's regulars, but Bolan had no reason to believe they would recognize him. Even if Captain Mansaré had informed them of their coversations, what would that mean if they met a stranger in the heat of battle?

Maybe nothing. But it ran against the grain for him to stand by on the sidelines, maybe giving General Diallo time to slip away in the confusion.

Bolan swapped his rifle for the RPG once more, sighted on a portion of the compound farthest from the open gate and fired. The rocket was still airborne as he snatched his FAL and broke from cover, sprinting toward the gate through darkness, like a shadow on the move. The warhead's blast drew every eye in that direction as he reached the gate, passed through it and found cover near the three Land Rovers that had brought Mansaré's men to join the fight.

From there, he saw Mansaré's party moving in the general direction that Diallo had to have run when Bolan lost him, soldiers here and there around the camp still firing toward the forest, others doubling back to intercept Mansaré and his men. The odds were still uneven, weighted on the army's side, and Bolan didn't want to see the new arrivals massacred after he'd called them to the party.

He could circle wide around them, leave them to their fate and try to find the general, or lend a hand where he was needed

at the moment. But maybe Mansaré's people would turn on him
with no idea that he was on their side.

Damn it!

The ring of troops was closing tight as Bolan raised his rifle,
index finger taking up the trigger slack.

ISMAEL DIALLO RAN as if his life depended on it—which, in fact,
it did. Fighting the dizziness that made his head swim, fearing
any moment that a bullet would rip through his back and bring
him down, he ran. Across the camp he fled, until he reached
the fence, then turned right automatically, jogging along with
chain-link on his left, knowing the fence would lead him without fail to find the gate, smashed open by whoever had arrived
to join the fight brief moments earlier.

They had to be enemies, since he had called no reinforcements of his own to help. Official-looking vehicles and men
in uniforms; it had to be the damned Judicial Police, perhaps
alerted somehow to the fact that he had grabbed their undercover man. They were too late to save him, but the fools still
might try to avenge him if they found Diallo.

If they lived that long.

He'd leave them to his soldiers, use the cover of their skirmish to escape while time remained. Once through the gate,
Diallo knew that he could reach Ponta Gardete without difficulty, moving through the forest with the access road to guide
him. In the town, he'd commandeer a vehicle and drive himself to Bissau, barricade himself inside headquarters. He would
be safe there, with his troops and tanks around him, while he
sorted out the damage from this night's fiasco.

Diallo saw the flattened gate ahead, heard firing on his right
flank and glanced back to see the uniformed invaders dueling
with his soldiers, muzzle flashes lighting up the night. Clutching the pistol he had used to kill Medina, ready at a second's
notice to defend himself, the general passed through and out
into the night, merging with shadows as he fled.

BOLAN'S FIRST SHOT dropped a shirtless soldier armed with an RPK light machine gun, just as his mark fired a burst toward Mansaré's small squad of police. The cops were all firing by then, taking down other regulars as Diallo's men turned on the threat they could see. Whether they thought the rival officers had shelled their camp or not, Bolan couldn't have said, nor did it matter now. In lieu of dueling with the forest, they would take what they could get.

And there were still enough of them to do the job.

Bolan shot two more gunners on the run, both falling in a mess of blood and tangled limbs. His gas mask didn't interfere with aiming, but it made his face sweat more than normal in the muggy, humid night. He couldn't wipe his forehead without breathing in the heady mix of coke and smoke he'd spread over the camp, and while a breeze was starting to disperse it now, he left the mask in place.

Another soldier down with one shot, on his right flank, as the mark was setting up to rake Mansaré's party with an RPD machine gun. The old Russian weapon had a funny look about it, like something from a fifties sci-fi movie, but the hundred 7.62 mm rounds in its drum magazine were man-killers, all the same. Half of them were gone now, as the dying soldier toppled over backward, firing at the stars.

One of Mansaré's people spotted Bolan then, was turning with his rifle shouldered when an army round took out the left side of his skull. One second he was aiming at the Executioner; the next, dead meat collapsing to the earth. Bolan spotted his killer, angling for another shot, and cut him down before he had a chance to make it two for two.

Diallo's soldiers had regained enough composure by that time to mount a final charge against their enemies in uniform, still missing Bolan on the sidelines where he crouched beside the Land Rovers. They came on like a banzai charge of old, shouting and weapons blazing, with Mansaré's people fighting for their lives at odds of two or three to one.

Bolan hurled frag grenades against the charging line and saw the blasts slash through the ranks, Mansaré's shooters making up the difference. The cops were taking hits, too, couldn't help it in the circumstances, but the ones who'd stretched prone to fire their auto rifles whittled down the other side. Bolan was busy at the same time, spotting individuals, leading his moving targets, squeezing off, then tracking on before they fell. He didn't count—had never been much into keeping score—but simply fired until the only targets still erect had dropped their guns and raised their hands.

A smoky silence settled over General Diallo's compound, with the man himself still nowhere to be seen. Bolan maintained his cover, watching as Mansaré took control, sending his uninjured survivors out to cuff and frisk the soldiers they had spared. There were too many for the Land Rovers, but Bolan guessed Mansaré had already thought of some alternative for carting them to jail.

What jail? It was the captain's problem. As for Bolan…

He saw one of the "dead" men stir behind Mansaré, rising on his elbows to extend a pistol toward the captain's back, unseen. The shot from Bolan's FAL cut through the silence, drilling the shooter's skull and bringing every eye around to his position. He rose, the rifle dangling at his side, and raised the gas mask with his left hand to reveal his sweaty face.

Mansaré gaped at him, began to say, "Are you—"

"We need to talk," the Executioner replied.

Epilogue

"I tell you, I barely escaped with my life," General Diallo said.

"You were fortunate, then," Pascal Kinte replied. "More Agwa de Bolivia?"

Diallo nodded, holding out his glass for a refill. He quaffed the coca-leaf liqueur greedily, as if he'd had nothing to drink for days and it was sweet, pure water. Seated in the recreation room of Kinte's lavish home, he tried to let the alcohol and coca soothe his agitated nerves.

"You say I'm fortunate!" Diallo answered. "I have lost three dozen men, two shipments of cocaine and the media—"

"Will soon forget all this and move along to something else," Kinte said, interrupting him. "You must regain perspective, General."

"I *have* perspective. The reporters make me out to be a gangster and a fool!"

"One part is true, you must admit," the minister replied. "As to the other, you can only prove them right by acting foolish."

"If I wanted your advice—"

"You do," Kinte said. "Why else are you here?"

"All right," Diallo grudgingly admitted. "What do you say I should do?"

"Ignore the media for now, and take decisive action to suppress your enemies. Show them your strength is not diminished. Be a *leader*."

"I *am* a leader," Diallo snapped. "Don't forget who you are speaking to!"

Kinte responded with a smile and said, "Now that's more like it. Show the fire you're known for. Hide from no man."

That was humorous, Diallo thought, with half a dozen guards outside Kinte's thirty-room mansion, furnished in style with state funds he'd embezzled. Still, the minister had managed to survive through several changes of regime in Guinea-Bissau and continued raking in the spoils, which proved that his advice was sound.

"How is your appetite, my friend?" Kinte asked.

"It depends on what you're serving," Diallo said.

"Only the best, General, as you've come to expect."

Kinte pushed a button on the intercom that occupied a corner of the lounge's hand-carved coffee table, alerting his servants that he and Diallo were ready for dinner. A moment later, the door opened behind Kinte and two men entered. One was African, the other white, and both held semiautomatic pistols tipped with sound suppressors.

Diallo thought about the little Walther PP pistol tucked inside his belt, beneath the jacket of his uniform, and knew he'd never reach it. Kinte saw the stunned expression on Diallo's face and half turned in his armchair, squeaking out a startled sound.

"Sorry we didn't meet last night," the white man told Diallo.

"This is for Nilson Medina and our country," the African said.

Diallo might have answered, given time, but there was no time left. As he went for his gun, both pistols made chugging sounds, three shots apiece, then silence ruled the house until a car started outside and quickly pulled away.

Osvaldo Vieira International Airport

"I'm not sure what to say in such a situation. Should I thank you for my life or warn you to stay out of Guinea-Bissau?"

"Either one or both," Bolan answered Captain Mansaré. "Maybe neither. Take your pick."

"It's better that you don't come back, I think," Mansaré said.

"I don't plan on it," Bolan said. "It's my first time leaving anywhere with a police escort."

"I owed you that, at least," Mansaré said. "A takeoff without difficulty."

"What about yourself?" Bolan asked.

"Oddly enough, it seems that I may be promoted. Or perhaps cashiered. I'll take whatever comes."

"I think your country needs you," Bolan said.

"Others may disagree. We'll see."

"About Medina…"

"Say no more. He made his choice and died unbroken. Few of us can say that, in the end."

A disembodied voice announced boarding for Bolan's flight. He shook hands with Mansaré, left the captain standing in the middle of the concourse and moved out toward his gate without a backward glance. There was nothing to hold him here except more ghosts.

He was leaving Guinea-Bissau more or less the way he found it, shaken up a bit but still not ready, in his estimation, to clean house. And if its mess slopped over to the States again, Bolan knew that he might be back. How would Mansaré take it, if that happened?

They would have to wait and see.

New battlegrounds were waiting for the Executioner. New predators.

War without end.

Amen.

* * * * *

TAKE 'EM FREE
2 action-packed novels
plus a mystery bonus

NO RISK

NO OBLIGATION
TO BUY

James Axler
Outlanders®

COSMIC RIFT

Dominate and Avenge

Untapped riches are being mined on Earth—a treasure trove of alien superscience strewn across the planet. High above, hidden in a quantum rift, the scavenger citizens of Authentiville have built a paradise from the trawled detritus of the God wars. A coup is poised to dethrone Authentiville's benevolent ruler and doom Earth, once again, to an epic battle against impossible odds. Cerberus must rally against a twisted—but quite human—new enemy who has mastered the secrets of inhuman power….

Available in November wherever books are sold.

GOUT67